APOTHEOSIS:

A TREATISE AGAINST
THE ELEVATION OF MAN

Nathaniel James Hood

APOTHEOSIS: *A TREATISE AGAINST THE ELEVATION OF MAN*

© 2021, Nathaniel James Hood.

Print ISBN: 978-1-09837-006-0

eBook ISBN: 978-1-09837-007-7

This book is dedicated to great contradictions,
to the things that make our heads spin, to a God
who can't fit in my little boxes, and to Audrey, who
accepts me as I am and still encourages me to grow.

Additionally, thank you to Cyrus Youngman,
Christopher Suder, and Andy Cassler for being
the first to consume these words, Matt Panfil for the
cover, and to my editor, Sharon Honeycutt,
who somehow managed to preserve my voice
without letting me sound like a total maniac.

CONTENTS

"Lean not on your own understanding."

PROVERBS 3:5B

CHAPTER 1:

A SIGNIFICANT DAY

THE DAY BEFORE A significant day seems like nothing to be cherished. No dire decision must be made. No chance must be taken. Life carries on casually without consequence or concern. With repercussions minimal, money is made and money is spent and all that matters is the simple passing of the hours. Then a significant day comes along. The insignificant day suddenly becomes wasted time. The ramifications of a decision that may have seemed to have meant absolutely nothing the day before become much more substantial. Weight arrives upon unsuspecting shoulders, and many of those shoulders collapse. One spilt beer can make for the greatest party that 1.2 million people have ever attended. One heart is broken, and the entire population of a greater metropolitan area ceases to exist. A gift becomes a curse. These, of course, are very specific examples.

The day before the most significant day in history was a good day for many people. Then again, perhaps the day before the significant day was actually the significant one. The inanity of its events made it seem otherwise, but, without those events, things would not have occurred as they did. So perhaps there are no insignificant days. Perhaps there is only the illusion of an insignificant day. Perhaps the notion of the mundane helps people think they are prepared for excitement. They can reserve their strength, their anxiety, their volition for the big event. If they had only kept sharp, however, they may have been more prepared. After all, an unused muscle deteriorates. Perhaps the realization that there are no insignificant days allows a man to remain limber and poised, ready to react at a moment's notice. Maybe if the Ripple Six had treated every day with fervor, they would have been more prepared for the events that would lead to the end of the world.

On the day before what seemed to be the significant day, Chester and Arch were getting high in their apartment, as they did most days. This is how insignificant people make insignificant days a little more significant – assuming there are insignificant days at all. It was about four in the afternoon, and Erin was there too. She only smoked when the guys did, and Chester and Arch were pretty committed to the lifestyle.

Erin had never been much more than a reflection of the people surrounding her, but every group of friends does well to have a mirror in it as a mirror makes the rest of the group feel good about their strengths and positive qualities. (Mirrors also make the rest of the group view and potentially develop disdain for their own faults and failings if they have the good sense and humility to do so.) It was not that Erin lacked a personality. It was that she allowed her personality to be fluid to gain the favor of those around her; she cared enough about them to let them see themselves in her. It was a rather ingenious way to please people.

Damien and Madeleine were intertwined in the back bedroom, as they were more often than not. An observer might have a difficult time determining where one body ended and the other began. Damien and Madeleine had nearly reached the place where they could not either.

Immediately upon meeting, Damien and Madeleine formed a type of spiritual and emotional mutualistic symbiosis, a state of mutual benefit that occurs naturally when needs are met equally in two or more separate parties. Although both parties do fine before meeting each other, they quickly find that they benefit from and thrive in each other's company and with each other's cooperation. This was Damien and Madeleine.

Damien was a musician, and Madeleine was a photographer. They both saw life's varying guises and attempted to remove its masks and unlock truth through their own respective mediums. As was common for a musician, Damien saw darkness most places he looked, and this sadness seemed to write his songs for him. He found merit in melancholy. It was realism to him. He would not be blinded by bliss.

Madeleine saw beauty all around her. The untied shoe of a homeless man at the bus station was the perfect picture of a man who had scoured and scrounged, searching for the American dream. She saw a man who never stopped trekking, and though he may be down on his luck at the moment, he would never stop. At least he had a shoe to be untied, Madeleine thought, while Damien saw it as an indicator that no matter how long or hard you walked, life would untie your shoe over and over again.

Damien found solace in sadness. Madeleine found potential for positivity in something that was broken. Between the two of them, the vibrant, spinning world eventually settled into a certain shade of grey, one that seemed to them an all-encompassing understanding and ostensible state of peace. They grounded each other. Unchecked optimism can blind the eye to reality, and rampant pessimism can cripple the soul. Damien and Madeleine met each other between two worldviews and created a new one – one that could be had only by two people in communion with each other.

Off the coast of Laguna, a city in the south of Brazil, certain bottlenose dolphins have created a similar relationship with the local fishermen.

The dolphins corral schools of mullet into a closed-off area and notify the fisherman of their presence by slapping their tails on the water. The fishermen promptly move to the location and net the fish. Once the fish are immobilized, the dolphins pick them easily from the net and devour any stray fish with minimal effort.

In Ethiopia and Kenya, tribes of the Borana Oromo people, or Boran, have developed a similar relationship with the honeyguide bird that feeds primarily on the larvae and wax that they find in honeycombs. The Boran are only interested in the sweet honey that the bees create. The honeyguide birds are far more skilled at locating the bee colonies than their human counterparts, but extraction of their food source proves to be quite difficult. The Boran have no problem digging the honeycombs out once they have found the bee colony. These African people have developed a whistle to summon the honeyguide bird, and when it is blown, the honeyguide leads the Boran to the nearest source of honey, wax, and grub. It does not leave its human companion behind in the journey to the bee colony, knowing that it needs the humans to effectively extract the honeycombs. Once the birds locate the beehive, the Boran people knock it down and break it open, making it easy for the birds to sift through the wreckage and find the delectable larvae they crave. The people can now harvest as much honey as they desire, thanks to the birds that led them there. Both parties gain something in each other's companionship.

Damien and Madeleine were the bottlenose dolphins and the fishermen. They were the honeyguide and the Boran. The dolphins and the fishermen both caught fish before they were introduced, but they caught much more working in tandem. The Boran and the birds harvested honey and food before they unified their efforts, but their search flourished in the company of each other. For an artist, inspiration is food. Where Damien and Madeleine had come across inspiration before, their unity seemed to yield unimaginable results. Though this all was true, their relationship was not exclusively pragmatic. Madeleine had a laugh that shined light into the darkest corners of Damien's soul. When Madeleine's world was spinning out of control, Damien seemed able to grab it with one unwavering hand and place it back where it needed to be.

"Listen to this," Damien said solemnly as he reached for an old, weathered and worn Moleskine notebook, tattered and torn over years of philosophical tussling.

I am creator. I am God.
So, I sewed your soul from straw.
I looked, I loved. Good, what I saw.
But coursing wind revealed your flaw.

And so I sculpted you from clay.
You managed to last for many days.
But the years passed by, brought you to decay.
Slowly you were unmade.

"What do you think?"

"I think I'm sad now," Madeleine sighed, which was how this conversation usually went. Her mood, her state of mind, and her life were all genuinely affected by his writing.

"No, but really," said Damien persistently.

Madeleine took her time. She never responded hastily to Damien's poetry.

"You think we should be unmade?" she asked. Light crept into the room from between the cracks in the blinds covering the window, giving them a small portion of light by which they could see each other and the world around them.

"In this poem, man is the creator and God is the creation," he said.

"Why would you make God out of straw?" Madeleine asked incredulously.

Damien looked at her. She was adorable. It was all he could do not to kiss her every time he saw her beautiful, freckled face. "I made God out of straw because it is what I had and I liked the way it looked," Damien explained. "If there is a god, it is something distant to us now. Something we must create for ourselves. Monotheistic believers tend to create their god out of stone. Stone is permanent and immovable. It gives no room for the belief to breathe. So, I made God out of straw. But straw could not hold up against opposition so I revised my creation. And, once again, I was forced to unmake it."

"Should you be making gods, Damien?"

"I have to! If it was clear what God was, everyone would agree on it. It would have shown itself to us by now. We would have a clear, unarguable picture of God, but as it is, we do not. We have to paint the picture for ourselves. I want to know what I am looking at more than anything but God seems not to care enough to show me," Damien said, becoming frenzied. As he spoke, he realized he was both questioning and answering, assured and clueless.

"For someone who claims not to know if there is or is not a god, Damien, you spend a great deal of time antagonizing the idea of it. I feel like that is dangerous. If you see something that you think is a sleeping bear in the woods, do you walk up and poke it to see if it is asleep?" She knew she had a point. "I would not. I would just admire it from afar and let it go on sleeping."

Damien did not respond immediately. He gave a bit of thought to this idea. "I think I would poke it," he said.

"No, you wouldn't. Why?"

"To see if it's actually a bear."

This is how it was with them, and it was good.

At this point, Peter was arriving at the apartment. A record of a muddled genre spun seamlessly in the corner. The voice of a young Jewish gentleman escaped the speakers, singing misguided, self-absorbed, yet incomparably perceptive commentary on his own apathy. The melody was sanguine, the singer's voice abrasive. This coarse vocal styling was essential for this band's particular fan base. Without it, the music would be too accessible, too listenable. The lyrics were poetic and insightful, the choices in instrumentation enlightened and relatively reachable. Every cadence made for a record that a mother of three could listen to in her minivan as she dutifully picked up her eldest from soccer practice, but no soccer mom listened to this record. That voice, that sonic sandpaper, unsettling as it was, gave its hearers hope that the dirtiest, most down-trodden people could be insightful, inspired, and artistic. There was no smoke, no mirrors, no auto-tune, just truth delivered by the unlikeliest of troubadours.

Peter entered the apartment and was bombarded by smoke, laughter, and the sounds from the record player. Peter, like Damien and Madeleine, was a spiritual kid. For Peter, nothing was insignificant. Every occurrence had cosmic consequences. The day before Peter quit smoking cigarettes, he bought a blue pack of American Spirits, and the cash register displayed the price, $6.66. The pack of cigarettes cost six dollars and sixty-six cents. It was as if the Lord Himself had descended from His throne on high and possessed that cash register in Indianapolis to speak to Peter directly. Peter panicked and returned to his car, sweating from his anxiety. For weeks prior, he had been considering quitting, going back and forth on the pros and cons of continuing a relationship with cigarettes. Now, on a suddenly significant evening, he had his answer. Those numbers on the cash register told Peter that cigarettes were from and for the devil.

Luckily for Peter, he had his own numbers. The Lord created the world in seven days, and Peter would create a new world for himself using the same number. He immediately removed thirteen cigarettes from the blue pack, broke them in half with an unbridled level of conviction, and threw them away. Everything made sense to Peter in this moment.

Biblically, thirteen was a symbol of rebellion. The dragon, Satan, is mentioned thirteen times in the book of Revelation. Nimrod, thirteenth in the line of Ham, one of three sons of Noah, was infamously rebellious. His name was derived from the Hebrew verb "marad," which means "to rebel," and it is believed that Nimrod was responsible for establishing the kingdom of Babylon, within which the tower of Babel was found. Peter wanted no part in the Tower of Babel and he wanted no part in rebellion against the Lord and he wanted no part in the number thirteen. By breaking thirteen cigarettes that evening, he was rebelling against rebellion itself. This left him with seven cigarettes.

Like in the seven days of creation, a new world would form in Peter's heart over the course of those seven cigarettes. Like the seven trumpets blown by the seven priests around the walls of Jericho, he puffed on those cigarettes with vigor, and the walls of his addiction crumbled. This night occurred one hundred and thirty-eight days before what seemed to be the day before the significant day, and Peter had not smoked cigarettes since.

Pot makes you hungry and so does intertwining, so by now, everyone in the apartment was ready to eat. Damien and Madeleine emerged triumphantly from the back bedroom, and Damien asked if anyone wanted to go get food. He was answered with the excited eyes and smiles a child holds on Christmas morning. Food would be such a treat.

The gang put on their shoes and jackets and stumbled into daylight. A soft, February sun met their shoulders so gingerly it was as if it was not there at all. Seen but hardly felt, it smiled their eyes and set them upon their way.

It had been a merciful winter thus far, snowing only thrice and never more than a few inches at a time. It was odd for Indiana. The meteorologists claimed that they were still in for some impressive, typical Hoosier winter weather despite the delay, but it certainly had not come yet. Old Man Winter had overslept and was late to his shift that year – or he was waiting on something. Save a couple stubborn leaves, the trees were completely barren. Considering the time of year, it was a strange miracle any foliage remained there at all, but like dinner guests holding on to an enjoyable evening as long as they could, a few leaves lingered.

The group decided on an Indian buffet at the end of a strip mall about three blocks away as their dinner destination. It was one of the most consequential decisions any of them had ever made, though they were oblivious to this fact. The soles of their shoes began consuming the pavement, and their laughter filled the air.

As the Ripple Six traveled down the sidewalk, one solitary, miraculously remaining leaf, a last bastion of the past seasons, decided it was its own fateful time to fall and separated itself from its tree, landing noiselessly in the hood of Damien's jacket. Madeleine pulled it out and held it in her hand for a minute. In the dehydrated veins of that leaf was a dead season. She saw proof that those days were gone but not forgotten and lived in her memory for a moment. The leaf told her that the past had happened, but that it had to go. Each season must give way to its successor. The world must keep on spinning, setting the stage for life and death. The ebb and flow of creation and destruction sat, encompassed in a moment in her palm, and she gave thanks for all of it. All would soon be dead and born again. All would soon be dead and born again. All would soon be dead and born again. Right now, they were dying.

They made it to the Indian buffet and piled their plates with naan, rice, chicken dishes, and various spicy curries and chutneys. Their bellies filled and the laughter continued and right next door was a store they would soon enter, a store that held something either eternally unfunny or cosmically laughable. Maybe it was both.

They paid their checks and exited the restaurant, once again inviting the last rations of sun for the day to their shoulders. Arch had put on sunglasses to shield his lowered gaze. He spun around just like the world was doing under his feet. He had not planned the spin, but it could be said that something did. Maybe it was God. Maybe it was Charles Darwin. Maybe it was little green men who had planted antennae in the spine of every man and controlled them like RC cars from a planet far away. Who planned it did not matter. Why, at the moment, did not either. Where and when were the operative questions.

The spin slowed, and Arch found himself staring at a tattered sign above a dingy storefront that read "Yesterday's Folly Antiques" in rotting wooden letters and chipped paint. Arch read it aloud. "We should go in there," he said, and they did.

CHAPTER 2:

YESTERDAY'S FOLLY

A BELL RIGGED TO announce arrivals to the antique store rang as they stepped inside. An old woman with a strong back and a fretful brow stood behind the front desk. A man, slightly younger, equally weathered, leaned against the counter across from her, his seemingly careless posture betrayed by the tension in his shoulders, the severity in his gaze, and the lines around his eyes. Of the things he had earned in his many years on Earth, carelessness was not one of them. Thick glasses sat on the tip of his nose and were connected around the back of his head by a strap. The old shopkeeper looked upon the motley crew as they entered and gave them a hearty smile.

"Please come in. But be careful. A lot of this stuff is old and breakable … including me!" At this, the old couple shared a laugh. Fully aware of how tough they really were, how much had failed to break them over the years, the elderly couple were able to joke about their fragility. Both were far stronger-willed than any of the kids entering the shop that day, but they assumed a humble role, selling modest antiquities to the cocksure, the frivolous, the stoned, cracking wise about their breakability. They were the product of a better generation quietly evaporating from space and time.

Peter was the first to respond. "Mind if we look around? We were next door and ..." He found himself overexplaining, as he often did, and trailed off as the old woman smiled and held up her hand.

"Not at all, sweetheart," the old woman replied. As a septuagenarian with decades of human observation beneath her belt, she was immediately able to see him as the kind boy he was, a kind boy who reached a bit too far outward, a boy disposed by his own dutifulness.

They spent some time wandering about. Madeleine turned a lamp on and off a few times. Arch flipped through a few old records. Erin put on an old dress and spun around, the hem of it dancing and twirling and brushing against her ankles, making her happy. Peter looked on. She truly looked beautiful and free in that moment. He smiled. They simply explored, acting in the antique store in a way indicative of their entire lives. They looked for nothing in particular and hoped to find something special. Believe it or not, on this day, they did.

Damien moved methodically throughout the store. Each step was intentional, though the lines he walked were far from straight. He would amble near a friend, and as they turned to see him, he would shift his gaze away and walk in a new direction. He picked up trinkets that matched his personality and put them back down. He looked at everything and saw nothing at all.

Slowly, certainly, he made his way to the dimly lit tail of the store where colors were faded and dust had accumulated on most of the shelves. It was the part of the antique store that time forgot. Because it was a big store chockablock with curiosities, patrons of Yesterday's Folly usually had their attention claimed or lost far before they made it this far back. Damien, characteristically paying attention to little more than the contents of his own head, found himself in uncharted territory.

The walls in the back room were more picture than actual wall. Old frames held old prints, and reproduction paintings, outnumbering the occasional original work, sneaked in amidst the rest. The subject matters of the paintings were from a different era and profoundly uninteresting to young Damien. A young child received a haircut in one picture. A group of young British lords hunted a fox in another. One sepia-toned photograph showed a family standing solemnly and silently. They had stood there for decades. On top of that, it had probably felt like decades passed when they were getting that picture taken. It took a long time to take a photograph in 1897. No one smiled because no one could hold a smile that long. Dental hygiene was far from a priority at the time, and a sober face was thought to look wealthier. One child's face was slightly blurred.

Sleepy eyed, Damien remained in his fugue state as he scanned the wall.

All is old

All is new

Nothing changes

Nothing stews

I am slumber

Woke anew

I sleep enthused

In grey, in blue.

Suddenly, like a shout, he was startled awake. One solitary item reached from the wall with an iron grip and grasped his attention. He was suddenly in the apex of awareness, plucked from his stupor by a map.

It was a map of the world much unlike any other he had ever seen. It was about three or four feet wide and two or three feet tall. Yellowed and used, it seemed as old as the world itself, as antique maps often do. It was remarkably detailed. The mountains were drawn with perfect snowcaps and shadows. The rivers and oceans seemed to almost flow across the page. Damien could not avert his gaze. He scanned the countries, the cities, the rivers. *I know that one. I know that one. I have never heard of that one. What a strange name.* He scanned with great focus, completely enraptured by the map. The longer he stared, the more he slipped from consciousness. The steely hands of attention grasped and held his head and fixed his face toward the map. He traveled the earth in that moment, living as a nomad in his own mind, traversing the peaks, the valleys, the oceans, the coasts. The terrain fell victim to his darting eyes and unplumbed imagination. He saw a mountain goat skipping about the rocks of the Himalayas. He saw a pod of blue whales breaching the skin of the Atlantic. Warlords took what was not theirs, and he kept moving along. He saw tigers, tornados, beauty and beast. He saw hunger and sadness and fat folk spending twelve dollars and ninety-five cents on a cheeseburger with peanut butter on it. He saw newborn babies cry and volcanoes explode. He saw flowers bloom and then close. He saw every step of the cycles of life and death in a single moment.

Then he came to the end of his journey, the edge of the world, and found it curious. Along the edges of the map were burns, cuts, and frays, but nothing substantial, nothing that had reached the geographical detail within the borders save a gash in the Pacific and the Southwest United States. As if this map had survived many attacks. As if this map, just like the earth it portrayed, had some sort of innate talent for survival. Damien did not realize he had not broken his gaze for many minutes as he stared slack-jawed at the wall. The map seemed to shimmer in the dimly lit dusk of the back room of Yesterday's Folly.

"Dude."

Damien leapt as the single word crept into his consciousness. Arch, at some point in Damien's enamor, had crept up behind him, completely unknown to Damien, and begun speaking.

"Pretty cool map, yeah?" Arch said.

"Look at it," Damien dryly replied. Arch complied, and his eyes were pulled past the side of Damien's head and fell upon the map. He started to feel drawn in himself.

"It is really cool, man."

"I think I might get this," said Damien.

"Whatever blows your skirt up," said Arch, silently understanding the attraction. Damien reached forward and pulled the map off the wall, and the room seemed to shiver. The young men both scowled but said nothing to each other, secretly doubting they had felt the tremor at all.

Damien and Arch made their way to the checkout counter, gathering the rest of the group as they moved. Damien held the map by the top of its thin, wooden frame. Though it was surprisingly light, the mere size of it started to cause his arms to shake a bit.

"I would like to purchase this," he said to the weathered, wizened, old woman.

"Oh, that is a very nice piece," she sincerely replied, setting it up on the counter and looking it over. "Very nice," she repeated. They exchanged far too little currency for far too great a good, not knowing fully the significance of what they were selling nor what they were buying.

"That has been here a long time. I do not know much about its origin, but I know it is old. Decades and decades, I believe. A young man brought that in. Black hair. A little older than you." She closed her eyes when she spoke, drawing out her words to buy herself time before she had to complete her thoughts. "He was handsome, like you, and said it had been in his family for many years. Many years. He sold it to me for cheap. That's why you're getting it at such a price. He seemed just to want someone else to have it. I am glad it has found its home." She winked, and Damien, who had blushed a bit when she called him handsome, turned a slightly deeper shade of red.

The old woman's editorializing was hardly necessary. She had already made her sale. But she loved her merchandise and Damien loved the map, so she talked and he listened. He thanked her, and they left the store, taking the map with them.

CHAPTER 3:

A DROP OF BEER

ON THE WALK HOME from Yesterday's Folly, the whole world seemed to hum, as if existence itself was shifting, inhaling and breathing out. Electricity surged throughout it all, and anticipation heightened in the souls of the sidewalks and the cars that passed and the drivers of those cars and the cold air and the kids walking home. The universe vibrated in a way that seemed to say, "Change is going to come."

Within a few minutes of home, the party decided to split. The sun was setting, and that meant it was time to drink. Chester and Arch turned left toward the liquor store, and everyone else pointed themselves toward the apartment. The beer pong table needed to be set up. A playlist needed to be made. Frivolity needed preparation. On top of that, Damien needed to hang his map.

Chester and Arch arrived at the apartment about thirty minutes after the rest, their arms full of libations. For earlier in the evening, when their taste buds would still be functioning, they had pretentiously titled microbrews with pun-based names that involved combinations of beer ingredients and a political figure or a time of the year. Then a case of Hamm's for later when taste hardly mattered as much. Things seemed to be underway. A few friends had arrived, and smoke was filling the air again. They both were and were in the presence of self-appointed bohemian royalty. Chester and Arch knew what to do. Well acquainted with headless hedonism, they loosened their lips, cracked their beers, and engaged the guests.

It was dizzying listening to them talk. Words spilled aimlessly out of their mouths, their volume compensating for any lack of trajectory their words had. Anyone within earshot unwittingly became a listener, an involuntary sounding board, yet there was passion in every word too. Their lexis, their language seemed to shine for no apparent reason, calling into question whether worth could be appropriated to something completely useless. They had a joyful propensity for conversation, for noise.

They were masters in musing, despots in discussion, tyrants in talk. A listener was automatically instilled with interest and could not, no matter how they tried, tell you why. One of their conversations was so inebriating that an observer would leave feeling full without realizing that they had not learned, heard, or said a single thing. And if there was nothing to talk about, they would still talk – about nothing. They made up for a lack of content with charming little Midwest idioms like "madder than a smashed cat," "born in a barrel," and "don't judge a fish by how well it can climb a tree."

Currently, they were prattling on about a billboard they had seen off I-465 that depicted rabbits gambling at Indiana Grand Casino.

"Rabbits love gambling. Everyone knows that," Chester said with the confidence of someone speaking about the laws of physics.

Arch ran his mouth, trying to find a way to create a pun out of "carrot" and "baccarat." He failed miserably, but those listening were still delightfully enraptured.

Damien smiled to himself and thought, *This is why we keep them around.* Most of their humor was esoteric, and it was about eleven times funnier to those that knew them personally.

Damien had centered the map carefully on the wall behind the couch as soon as he got home. It took him about five minutes. Using his dad's level and stud finder that he had borrowed and never given back, he found three studs perfectly in line with each other. The map was strategically placed so that anyone in the main section of the apartment could view it. Little did they know, it was more like the map was watching them, waiting, anticipating their fateful rulings. They continued to live without consequence, unconsciously carrying all of it upon their shoulders. When Chester got there, he grabbed the stud finder, held it up to his own face, made a beeping sound, and winked at Damien.

"Alright," said Damien.

A game of beer pong was proposed, and Erin, Peter, Damien, and Madeleine took to the table. The first game turned into something of a tournament after Damien and Madeleine took the first win.

"Best two out of three? Come on." Peter was not going to go down so easily. A few beers deep, the cups began to dance and trade distance, as if they were bending the space and time they occupied. Luckily, this was not the first time they had seen reality dance around them. They knew how to dance with it. They knew how to bend their bodies, squint their eyes, and navigate inebriation with an acuteness that only came with experience.

Peter found it funny to reference relatively obscure, old NBA players every time he took a shot. He would shout, "Toni Kukoč, the Croatian sensation!" and "Greg Ostertag!" with elongated vowels. He did not know much more about the players than their names, but he found it funny and his friends seemed to as well. Damien laughed at about anything when he was drunk. He laughed so little during the day but so much after the hooch began to flow, as if he saved it for the night, afraid he might use it all up before the party started.

Erin and Peter had pulled into the lead and were up three cups. Erin was talking smack.

"I remember my first game," she taunted.

"No, you absolutely do not," Damien retorted.

"You're right," she laughed. They all laughed. Blackouts are a lot funnier at their age – before consequence, before crippling hangovers, before friends too hard to impress. This was an insignificant age. Either that or it was not.

Damien and Madeleine managed to eliminate a few more cups as the game progressed, but they could not seem to bridge the gap between Peter and Erin and them. It was becoming increasingly clear who was going to win and who was going to lose, but the losers were not losing heart. This game of champions, for most, was not about winning. Peter and Erin had one cup left, and Erin was up to bat. She squared her feet, raised her arm, and tossed. The ball glided through the air, a small amount of backspin affecting its trajectory. It hit the backside of the final red plastic cup and fell into the water.

Peter threw his arms into the air and yelled, and a few drops of beer flew out of the bottle he was holding. They flew silently behind him and through the air toward the wall behind the couch like a meticulously ordered drone strike. Cheers and laughter filled the air. One drop reached Damien's recently hung map and landed directly on the dot marked New Orleans. No one saw it happen.

CHAPTER 4:

WATER TO WEIZEN

THE FESTIVAL WAS ALL aflutter on the final night of Mardi Gras. Fat Tuesday was in full swing, and festivalgoers gave credence to the title. They filled their bellies in bestial bliss, converting calories to laughter, that special kind of laughter that they would know had happened the following day but would not for the life of them remember why. Specifics faded into the ether, and they seemed happy.

Not a single person at the party in New Orleans knew that they were about to be in the epicenter of the most significant meteorological and mystical event so far in history. They thought the most momentous things that could happen that evening would be shots shared with friends, an amazing photo taken with people in masks, or the possibility of taking someone back to the hotel. As it is with most events this tremendous, they often fall on unsuspecting shoulders.

Teddy, whose name is hardly important – or is immeasurably important – was the first to notice the rain. He felt a solitary drop fall on his left arm.

"Hey, guys. Let's find a bar. It's starting to rain," he mentioned to his comrades as he wiped it away. The liquid he wiped from his skin was thicker and stickier than any rain with which he was familiar. Another drop fell on the back of his right hand, and looking closely at it, he thought it seemed vaguely gold. Curious, he smelled it. Teddy furrowed his brow like Sherlock Holmes in the throes of a great investigation. He lapped it up. It tasted familiar, like the beverage he had been enjoying all night. As the amount of rain falling continued to increase, he looked around to see if it could be coming from anywhere but the sky, but that seemed to be the source. Although he could not be sure quite yet, he was starting to develop a hypothesis.

"Guys …" The word hardly left his lips before the sweet, golden liquid began to fill the air around them. It fell, and the smell permeated the air, so much thicker than before. There was no longer any doubt.

"It's beer!" rang an elated voice down the street.

Shouts of joy filled the air from all directions. Heads were thrown back, and tongues were thrown toward the heavens.

"What is happening!?"

"Can you believe it?!!"

"Deb! Look!"

"Here! Hold your cup up!"

"MARDI GRAS MIRACLE, Y'ALL!"

Teddy's hypothesis had become confirmed. The benevolent sky had apparently deemed them worthy of the greatest party the world had ever known and blessed them with a very special rain. The sky cried beer upon their eager tongues and filled their open mouths.

"I thought Jesus was supposed to turn water into wine!" laughed Teddy's friend Beth. Teddy cheered and raised an empty glass.

And they drank. All night long, a steady torrent of beer fell from the sky in New Orleans, and no one feared. They ran back and forth in the streets that night, their glasses raised aloft. Even the bartenders left their posts to take part in the holy water falling. In their heads and their hearts, God's providence was extended to them that night to provide them with incalculable inebriation, and they gulped it up unabated. *It must be good,* they thought, *because it was fun, because it was free, because it felt so good. It must be fine.*

The next morning, the headlines offered, "Miracle at Mardi Gras," "Water to Weizen," "The Drunken Downpour," and various other witty quips of the sort. The festivalgoers had made it back to their respective homes and hotels, drunk, full, and baffled – but not so baffled that they would be disappointed if the miracle were never explained. They were just happy they had been there, that it had happened. The streets had nearly flooded with the gilded liquid that evening, and most folks' clothes and shoes reeked of beer. Teddy pointed out to his friends toward the end of the night that the very streets of heaven were going to be gold. But, as so many Shakespearean scholars and so few millennials know, all that glisters is not gold.

CHAPTER 5:

THERE

THE RIPPLE SIX AWOKE around brunch time with foggy heads full of content and contentment. They were the only ones who stayed at the apartment that night. It was home base for them, whether they were one of the three tenants or not. Although Damien, Chester, and Arch were the only ones on the lease, Madeleine slept there a great majority of evenings, tethered to Damien's side, and Peter and Erin were regulars. They all wiped the crust and confusion from their midmorning eyes and shuffled to put on clothes that had not been washed. They were filled with joy to have their friends around them first thing in the morning. Menial conversation filtered through the air. They asked questions that began, "Do you remember ...?" and "When did we ...?"

They decided to go to Broad Ripple Bagel Deli, a favorite of Broad Ripple's hungover denizens, for breakfast and moved in a pack out the door. After about five minutes of foot travel, they arrived at the main strip of town. A bullhorned bellow filled their ears, the source two men, one younger, one older. The older man was shouting into the horn with a level of resolve and conviction rarely seen. The younger man, seemingly in the late high school or early college years of his life, seemed less sure of his self but seemed to gain confidence whenever he looked to the older man. As they walked past, this is what the Ripple Six heard:

"Mardi Gras did not receive blessings in the events of last night. They received retribution! For too long they insisted that drunkenness, promiscuity, and debauchery were to be their pleasure, their joy, their paltry gods. Now the real God, creator of the universe, has given them over to their devices! He has cast them from His bosom into a sea far less comforting than it seems or than they had hoped it would be! And there they shall float! In their iniquity! Without direction or hope of rescue! Forevermore!"

Arch, through a plume of smoke stolen from his cigarette, always first to talk, asked the obvious, "What is all of that about?"

He had not checked his Twitter yet that morning. He did not have enough caffeine and nicotine coursing through his bloodstream for that social swamp. Luckily for the group, the girls mainlined Twitter quickly after waking each morning.

Erin said, "Hold on. Let me check." She pressed the little bird on her phone as they walked into the bagel deli.

Her finger danced upward across the screen no more than a few times before she found the article. Damien had placed a hand on the small of Madeleine's back and guided her gently toward the counter to order a greasy, midmorning monstrosity.

"Oh my gosh. It's on everything. Here. It's on *Huffpost*. It's on everything." She scanned the article quickly. "Apparently, at Mardi Gras last night, beer fell from the sky."

"I'm sorry. Who, what, when, where and why?" said Arch.

"Yeah. It literally rained beer."

"You're reading *The Onion*."

"No. This is *Huffpost*. Look." She held the phone toward Arch, hand trembling a little. They all shook a little most of the time. She shook a little more than usual. This time, it was not from malnutrition or dehydration.

"It's on every news source."

"Ope. Yikes."

They all ordered their bageled sandwiches and found a table out back. It was a brisk February morning. They were still making small, strangely unexcited conversation about the beer storm.

"Straight up. This is what happened. The Mardi Gras board or whoever plans the festival flew a plane overhead and sprayed it down on all of them. You know how they spray pesticides over crops from those little planes? That's what they did." This was Chester speaking.

It is not important who said what for the next few lines. Not until Peter said something of extreme importance.

"Why would they do that?"

"Because party."

Laughter.

"That would lose them a lot of money."

"I'm sure they have it to spare. Actually, I don't know. Isn't the whole festival about spending money?"

Mouth sounds filled the air for a minute as they chewed.

"I bet it was the government. Chemtrails, dude. I bet there was poison in it. Population control."

"No one died."

"Yet."

"It could have been mind-control serum."

Laughter followed this comment.

"Or it could have been a delayed reaction."

"You're an idiot."

"Yes, I am."

"It happens every day."

"Mind-control serum?"

"Stuff like that."

More laughter was followed promptly by more mouth sounds.

"I think it was God like the guy said," Peter said and shrugged. After they had finished their various bageled sandwich monstrosities, their souls took sole once more, this time in the direction of their apartment. A bullhorned bellow again began to get nearer, and Madeleine felt a spirit take her. She reached down and plucked a small purple flower growing from a window box outside one of the bars they passed on the strip. When they reached the loud evangelist and his nervous young apprentice for the second time, she walked to the younger of the two and handed him the flower. A shy smile broke out across his face, and he thanked her. He looked to the older man who had stopped shouting momentarily. The old man gestured with his head to the pamphlets in the boy's hand and then to Madeleine. The boy handed her a tract promising an answer to sadness.

"Do you believe in Jesus?" he meekly asked her.

"I think so," she replied. "And I believe in you."

She winked and turned away from him quickly so that her hair spun out, misting him in a potpourri of the sweet, stale scents of her shampoo and perfume from the day before. He stood there with his tracts in his hand, flabbergasted by the single-greatest interaction he had ever had with any girl at all, much less a pretty one.

Before long, the Ripple Six arrived safely back at the apartment. Chester and Erin both had work that afternoon, so Chester briefly visited his bedroom to prepare and Erin headed straight home. Brief hugs and snarky goodbyes were shared. They had survived another night and were that much closer for it.

The remaining four shared in a bowl packed to the brim of that pungent, psychoactive plant they thought of so fondly and debated whether or not to play Mario Kart or watch *The Simpsons*. Amidst the deliberations, Arch adjourned to the kitchen, losing his vote. Mario Kart was decided upon in his absence, and they began to play. Damien was the quickest and secured Yoshi, who they all were convinced was the best character. He was moderately heavy, so he could hold his own in an altercation without compromising speed. Peter chose Toad, still believing that the fastest character was the one that would win. He sometimes had a hard time taking more than a few factors into account. Madeleine chose Princess Peach, as she always did, for she represented all things good and innocent, the way she hoped to see the world.

"I got next," Arch mumbled through a mouth full of chips and salsa as he re-entered the room.

After a few rounds, Peter began to feel a bit restless and suggested going to see a film. Neither Damien nor Madeleine showed much interest, but Arch was amenable. They put on their coats and stepped into the sun. Damien and Madeleine were alone together in the apartment.

Damien packed another bowl as Madeleine used the restroom and decided on watching *Life*, a critically acclaimed nature documentary program that they found infinitely fascinating together. He knew she would appreciate the choice. They smoked and took in the many wonders of the natural world through smiled eyes, dreaming of seeing them in person outside a forty-six-inch screen. They laughed at how the narrator pronounced the word "orangutan."

Madeleine thought of other places and of how beautiful those other places were. She began to, in her mind, subscribe to the idea that trouble and turmoil, peace and pleasure were all geographically specific. She thought that if she could take Damien somewhere else, he would be able to shirk the weights tethered so tightly to his heart, keeping his feet so close to the ground. She thought that she may be able to find more of the goodness that she so adamantly believed in than she currently found in her small city.

"Let's go somewhere," she blurted and grabbed Damien on the arm. Damien assumed this was apropos of nothing besides the playful mountain goats bounding across the television.

"Let's do it. Where do you want to go?" he said with equal parts detachment and affection, his personal brand of interaction. He smiled without opening his mouth or showing his teeth.

Madeleine began to remember stories her older sister had given her of a small town in the northeast of France, where the sunlight bathed the brick streets in a gold that told its residents that riches could not be held in a vault, in a leather wallet, in a pair of jeans. It was a place where the flowers bloomed 365 days a year, it seemed, and a smile was the status quo. It was a place where the pastel-pasted storefronts filled the hearts of its citizens with color and joy.

She raised herself to her knees and whipped around on the couch, facing the map, twirling her hair around her in another sweet-smelling, brunette halo. She focused her eyes and found the city she remembered hearing so much about: Colmar. She looked over at Damien and smiled, then placed a finger against the map, directly upon Colmar, and said, "Someday, I want us to live there."

CHAPTER 6:

COR DEI

DAMIEN AWOKE THAT NIGHT within a clutter of color and line. He was stuck in what could only be described as a mess of differently colored strands of some semi-tangible substance. He tried to distinguish some sort of pattern in the celestial stew, but there was none, and that was okay. It was beautiful. He began to swim, his face brushing against strands of indigo, vermillion, forest greens, and oceanic blues, all conceivable members of the color spectrum and some hues for which he had no name. As the vibrant, undefined strings of color touched and tickled his excited skin, he began to chuckle. The vast complexity of what he could only explain as an ethereal ball of yarn sent him on a voyage of intricate, oscillating emotion. His chuckles turned to tears, his tears to fears, his fears to courage, his courage to doubt, his doubt to strength, his strength to tears again. The answer to every inquiry his soul had ever had was given to him without words.

Damien swam deeper into the kaleidoscopic soup, swinging from line to line like a spectral Tarzan. The beautiful mess of this space was all that mattered anymore. It was God. It was him. It was both conundrum and solution, emptying and filling him a million times each moment. He wanted so badly to be involved in that breathtaking ball of yarn. He would do anything to know it more. He decided he had to move it into some sort of organizational system that he could understand.

In a desperate desire to make sense of the lovely mess, to be a part of it, he grabbed every string one by one. He began to separate them into their own little spaces so that he could analyze them alone, like someone would parse a sentence. He pulled and weaved and organized. And as he itemized each individual color, it seemed to lose some vibrancy. Then he grabbed a bright, golden thread and pulled with all his might, and it all started to change.

The strings began to tighten. Around him, the lines were becoming rigid. His limbs became tangled and were pulled in four different directions, as if he were being quartered by his new deity. Fear gripped him as he was stretched and pulled, no longer free and swimming, no longer happy and hopeful. The lines lost no color or vibrancy, but in their new configuration, one without freedom and flow, they were no longer beautiful. They restrained him. All he had wanted was to leave his mark, to play a part in the beauty, but it had turned on him and now held him tight.

He started to see the danger in structure. How the same components that once brought him immeasurable peace and joy could become something very different when organized, when they were not allowed to flow freely. He was so bored, so angry, so stretched, being able to see and recognize each line and color individually. He realized how pedantic it was to try to identify, to classify, to organize something complex and beautiful, and so he pulled that same operative string. The strings loosened. He would not try to organize anymore. He would let the ball be what it was and enjoy it and thank the heavens he was there. He need not affect it, organize it, nor understand it. He would only swim and smile.

He was falling alongside the strings as they relaxed and began to swirl again. The warmth of beauty and freedom swilled his soul again. His fall seemed to slow without hitting anything, and he swam again. The joy, the peace, the power – God was back now that He was allowed to breathe, uninhibited by jurisdiction.

And Damien woke up.

CHAPTER 7:

HUNCHED

IT WAS TORTURE TO have a hunch like this, to be pins and needles on pins and needles. Like hearing the home was burgled and knowing
the window was left unlocked after opening it last Saturday when the
sun shined bright. Like sending a text with that one incendiary sentence,
meant to be harmless but sure to burn in the recipient's eyes like a leaf
fire. Like a best friend's home burning down after a party where cigarettes
were blissfully smoked, some of which were certainly not stamped out.

Madeleine felt this weight today. She knew it was her fault.

The sun was out, and the wind whipped mercilessly. She sat on the
patio at a café called the Featherlight and edited photos on her laptop
computer. At one point, she ordered a beer. When it arrived, she lifted it
off the coaster to raise it to her pouted lips. The wind picked the coaster up
off the table and threw it to the fence against which her table was pushed,
an invisible force holding the coaster in place. It did not fall. She grabbed
it and set it back under her beer. The event meant nothing but felt like
everything. All was weird and magical and ominous and off today.

That morning, the news reported the second supernatural event that
would occur that week. A circle with a nearly five-mile radius that seemed
to center on and include the small, scenic town of Colmar in France had

been completely destroyed the evening before. Areas surrounding the circle reported a large, beige rod lowering from the heavens directly above the town and landing on Colmar with a deafening thud, flattening miles of earth like some fleshy hydraulic press. Notable features of the destroyer were a peach-colored exterior, large creases and fissures in its surface, and a shiny, grey plate at the tip facing north.

Madeleine looked down at the grey acrylic polish resting upon her fingernails.

She had never felt this way before. At this moment, she felt only fear, and she felt it so strongly that no other aspect of personality remained in her. She was only fear. It was like a whiteout spread across her soul.

And the devil, in the presence of opportunity, bent her soul toward control, a trick he knew well and affectionately. He would have her take things into her own hands. To this end, a city bus sporting a sign for a local community college drove past and displayed, in big block letters, "Take control of your own life." And a voice whispered, just as it had in a garden many years before, "You can put things right. You can make things the way they should be. You can be God."

Her hand moved instinctively to her phone.

"We need to talk. Now. I need you."

These eight words, spread out across the luminescent brick in her hand, left it and headed toward the luminescent brick in her boyfriend's pocket, which vibrated, left the pocket, and displayed the message to Damien. She could send messages great distances. All was magical today.

"Baby? What's up?" responded Damien.

She initially typed, "Meet me at the apartment," but then realized what waited for her there. She would not look upon that unconfirmed instrument of destruction quite yet. She was afraid of the temptation to find out whether her hunch had legs. With one more little finger she could find out. With one more simple movement she could know if she was Madeleine, destroyer of worlds. She deleted the words and replaced them with, "Can you meet me at the Featherlight?" The café where she sat, pretending to edit photos, void of all but fear.

The wind continued to whip and bluster around her. She did not know quite how windy it was when she decided to go there and sit outside. She could not help but see those invisible forces as a certain kind of beautiful, inconveniencing as they may be. She always tried to see unexpected surprises this way. She could plan and hope all she wanted, but life, God, whatever she decided to call it that day would continuously throw her curveballs. She knew this. And, up until the news reports that morning, she believed that there was nothing left but to call those curveballs beautiful. She believed it the only way to get by and stay happy. But this could not be beautiful. A town had been destroyed.

Damien grabbed his bike and backpack and headed her way. He was not busy with much when she texted. He started to think about that as he pedaled down the pavement. Maybe he did not do enough. Maybe he had too much free time. But he worked hard when he did work. Kind of. Maybe he should get another job. But he had to focus on his music. He was investing in the future. Things would pick up someday. Oh, to see outside time. To step out and walk past the individual moments like exhibits at a museum. Then he could know if he was making the right choice. What was right? What was wrong? This is right. Taking care of Madeleine was right. He hoped he would have the words. He pushed the brakes, stopped, and lit a cigarette before his head spun completely off his shoulders.

As he got closer to the café, he felt fine. Her texts were a tad disconcerting, but Madeleine had the tendency to make metropolises out of molehills. He supposed that she was having a hard time editing a photo for one of her clients and could not get the color palette right or that her mom was nagging her about considering getting her own place. Damien would put on his boyfriend hat, a well-worn and weathered garment, place her trembling hand in his unwavering one, and hold it until it steadied.

When Madeleine saw Damien walking down the outside aisle at the café toward her, she suddenly sat a bit straighter than before, as if someone had pulled her skin tight around her. He walked toward her with a slight hunch, a backpack hanging off one shoulder, jeans ripped at the knees and covered with about three weeks' worth of dust and grime, an orange flannel open to four buttons from the top, sharing the vision of a small patch of hair resting on the skin over his sternum. His long, greasy hair fell onto his shoulders. He walked toward her with dozed purpose. He was going where he was going and figured that he would get there eventually; he saw no reason to rush. His hunch got her thinking of her own hunch. His hunch was a lot like hers. He stood with a bend, burdened because he thought that he might have life all figured out, and he was afraid of that being a reality. Her spirit had this same posture.

Madeleine had often thought of Damien as her pilot light. There is something beautiful about a pilot light. It keeps burning even when it is not needed. A pilot light just stays there, steady, ready to ignite the moment it is called upon. Damien was her pilot light.

He got closer, and Madeleine shot to her feet and threw her arms around him. She squeezed the air from his torso, and as he inhaled, he smelled a sweet fragrance from her neck. They pulled away an inch, locked lips, and then looked at each other in earnestness.

Love, nebulous as it is, can be defined many different ways, one being this:

Love is the alignment of one's will with another's.

Perfect love occurs only when two or more separate parties allow their individually tailored wills to begin to merge together to form a separate, entirely new will. It is not complete compromise, nor is it complete

dominance from either side. It is complete cooperation. It is as two com-
panies merging, not one absorbing another. True, powerful, perfect love
requires both compromise and immovability when necessary from both
sides. This is perfect love, though it is far from the easiest version of love.
Consider a four-way stop in the Midwest. As four cars pull up, they
exchange smiles and nods. The soft Midwest sun shines on their necks,
and their children squeal gleefully from the backseat as a cartoon fish
finds his father. All the drivers desire safety for themselves and their
families and to reach their destination in time, but they also desire this
for the other cars. In their Midwest hospitality, they take turns scooching
an inch forward, occasionally waving each other ahead, taking more time
to make it through the intersection than one would outside the Midwest.
One car pulls forward a bit as the one to its left does as well, and then they
both make a reactionary stop. Then they both wave each other forward.
Then they both pull forward and have to make another reactionary stop.
Both drivers begin to feel a little annoyed. If they both lean too far toward
compromise, neither car will ever make it through the intersection. If
they both lean too far toward aggression, they will each simultaneously
give in to their frustration and crash into each other. So, in the effort of
painting a picture of perfect love, imagine they do this dance for a few
more seconds, each driver scooching forward a little and then braking
simultaneously with the other. Eventually, one driver must lean a bit more
into compromise while the other takes action, vowing that next time they
will allow the other driver to go first. They both do this in the interest of
mutual success. One has to go first for everyone to proceed, and if they
can accomplish this, they will all get through the exchange just fine. All
parties will come out on top, but just as it is with love, it could have ended
in disaster. The alignment of separate wills is far from simple. Sometimes
there is a crash. Sometimes everyone gets where they need to go.

"Damien, I have something to tell you …" And then there was love.
She did not immediately pull into the intersection. Her eyes traversed the

slightly sun- and cigarette-damaged skin that kept his bones in. She looked for a response, some guidance, some strength before she even posed the question. His eyes assured her it was fine to continue.

"I ..." There was another pause. And then there was love. This pause was shorter.

"I think I destroyed Colmar."

And then there was love. Damien lit a cigarette. "You didn't destroy Colmar."

"Listen. Last night I touched Colmar on your new map and said I wanted to move there and you said it sounded like a toothpaste brand. Do you remember?"

"Of course I do."

"Well, have you looked at the effing news?" A quick burst into the intersection. Swear words felt uncomfortable for Madeleine, like intruders on her quivering lips. Even now, she could not compel herself to swear.

Damien took a pause. He was caught off guard, aghast, agape. This was as close as Madeleine got to using foul language. And this was another reason why they worked. Damien swore like a sailor. Madeleine kept her mouth clean, which represented to Damien an innocence in her that he idealized. He, like so many sailors before him, had found his sober-mouthed beauty on the shore.

"No, baby, I have not looked at the news." And then there was love.

Damien took to Google and researched the devastation in France while Madeleine stared at her grey-tipped fingernails. He read countless accounts of the event, finding time and time again that the origin and identity of this heavenly destroyer was so far unconfirmed, but it had some distinguishing features: a peach-colored exterior, large creases and fissures in its surface, and a shiny, grey plate at the tip facing north. Some articles hypothesized that it was a finger. Some articles likened it to the event in New Orleans. Strange things seemed afoot.

"So, let me get this straight." And then there was love as she sat there, ready to be wrecked, in the middle of the intersection. "Your finger went into my map and destroyed an entire town."

"That's what I believe."

He did not pull forward. He would not devastate her as she sat there vulnerable. And then there was love.

Damien could not see Madeleine as a destroyer in any capacity, whether she had meant to or not. She did not move enough in the world. She did not push or pull. She simply watched. She was a conscientious observer. They had talked about this before. He was the same way. They did not capture moments. They only commented on them. In fact, it was impossible to capture a moment. One can only create a new moment combining the subject and object, past and present, in a new work of art. She created new moments on top of the moments she witnessed through her photography. She created moments compounded, building, never destroying.

They sat in silence for a minute. Murmurs swirled around the patio, some pertaining to Colmar, some not. The two could not hear much more than that one proper noun that seemed to sit smugly on their windpipes. Damien, long done with his last, lit two more cigarettes and handed one to Madeleine.

They discussed hypothetical ramifications of the event. She was concerned it could be traced back to her somehow. In her head, she saw police at her door that very night. Afraid someone would recognize her nail polish, she started picking at them feverishly. Damien convinced her there were millions of people wearing that shade. Plus, for someone to figure out that it was a finger, magnified thousands of times in size, pushed through a map in Indianapolis, would be miraculous. She worried they would find DNA at the site. They decided that authorities would not be able to test for DNA at the site because any DNA left would be so big it would be unrecognizable and untraceable.

"This would be the most insane, supernatural, unexplainable, bonkers-crazy thing that has ever happened. So far as I know. I mean, there may be witches and sorcerers doing stuff like this under the radar every day … I'm sure I don't know what all is happening or has happened but this seems up there," he rambled nervously.

"I know." And then there was love. She needed him to pull forward, to tell her what to do next.

Damien recalled the event in New Orleans a couple days back just like the articles did. He mentioned to Madeleine that it may be connected if what she thought about the map was true. There were two accounts of supernatural events since Damien brought the map home to his apartment.

"We can't just assume." The degree to which they were entertaining this as a possibility was a testament to their imaginations. "If you're right, and you usually are, we have a map that can affect the entire world."

"I know."

"But that's impossible."

"I know."

Damien pulled forward. "Let's run it by the gang."

They sat and puffed for another minute. No one needed to pull forward. No one needed to wave. They simply sat. They had made it through the intersection.

CHAPTER 8:

JEAN-LUC VERSTADT

WHEN THE FINGER CAME down and destroyed his hometown, Jean-Luc Verstadt was walking his French Mastiff, Mitzi, about three miles from the center of town. He had gone much farther into the countryside this day than he remembered ever going before. Something kept his feet stepping. Something imperceptible kept calling him farther and farther from the bustling cobblestone streets that weaved agreeably through the small town of Colmar.

First, he heard the rip. It was like a pair of jeans had been split into a public announcement system somewhere high and huge in the atmosphere above. Then, before he could turn, he felt a rushing wind from above tousle his chestnut hair and push down on his shoulders. Mitzi barked.

As Jean-Luc turned, a shadow covered him, and a massive, beige wall came into his field of vision. Mere inches from himself and Mitzi was a wall lowering from the heavens, bigger than he could quantify, familiar in a way he could not put a finger on, more horrible than he could ever imagine. It lowered and impacted the earth directly in front of him and his slobbering companion, and the earth shuddered. Another forceful wave pushed outward and past him. He struggled to keep his footing.

Jean-Luc battled to believe himself as he reached forward and placed a hand upon the wall moments after it impacted. It felt so horribly familiar. He pushed forward into it, and it succumbed slightly to his effort, reminding him immediately of his own flesh. He leaned, slack-jawed, into it.

Then, quick as it came, the wall began to ascend back into the heavens. Jean-Luc watched it rise until the sky seemed to swallow it and it was gone. His eyes found their way back to the earth ahead of him. It was flat. For as far as Jean-Luc could see, where once sat a beautiful, historic, painted town called Colmar, was nothing but a level plane.

Jean-Luc Verstadt had been waiting for something. For twenty-four years he had lived in a town nearly conjured. Colmar resembled the most idyllic of fantasies. A photograph of the tiny utopia would be nearly indistinguishable next to the most paradisiacal painting by the most ethereal-minded artist the world could provide. But Jean-Luc found himself wanting. There had to be more than aesthetic. There had to be more than tradition. There had to be more.

His German father and French mother had moved to Colmar in the late seventies, attracted to the town by Christian Democracy and pastel-painted storefronts. Jean-Luc was born shortly after they settled, was raised in a loving household, and wanted for nothing. His mother baked bread, and his father collected matryoshka dolls. His home was multicultural, and he found a spread comfort in many different ideas. He was given an expansive homeschool education and grew into a bright young man. He ended up working at a small bakery in town, creating wonderful breads just as his mother had taught him.

Every night he would come home to his small, one-bedroom apartment, have a beer or two, and paint. He would turn the television on so that it hummed in the background, often turning the receiver to a gameshow. *Jeopardy* was like child's play to Jean-Luc, and he would often provide the questions without even looking up from his easel. But he wanted for something. There had to be something more than knowing the answers, than perfect, painted walls and the sweet smell of bread. There had to be more than human history. There had to be more than himself. Every evening, Jean-Luc's soul pushed outward.

When Jean-Luc realized that his home was gone, he did not feel sad. This was exactly the thing for which he had been waiting. He and Mitzi took off from the place where they had miraculously been missed and headed in the direction of his aunt and uncle's farmhouse, just two miles away. They had a notebook. When he got there, his aunt was wailing on the front porch, and his uncle was holding her. He breezed past them. His uncle shouted after him, and Jean-Luc paid him no mind. He scurried around the house until he found a small notebook and a handful of writing utensils. He ran back out of the house, past his grieving kin, and returned to the place where he had just survived extinction.

Jean-Luc's pencil took to the pages of the notebook like a fire catching hold. It started slow and moved faster and faster as the moments flew by. He wrote about the inability to know anything for certain and the likelihood that one's understanding of how things are would be obliterated without notice. He wrote about the beauty in destruction and how sorrow must be met upon some so that others may find delight. He wrote about how he had been chosen and how destruction had passed in front of him by inches. On the last pages, he wrote about something greater that he would never understand, but that seemed to understand him. His pencil worked furiously until every page of the notebook had been filled. He stopped, realizing he was sweating despite the cold air that now surrounded him. He looked over at Mitzi, and she stared straight back.

Jean-Luc opened his phone and found articles about the incident and pictures from afar of the beige destroyer he had just encountered. From a more distant perspective, it seemed almost like a human finger. His heart was filled with delight. He opened his notebook again, and at the top of the first page, he wrote:

The First Church of the Finger of God

As the days went by and people flocked to the land where Colmar once sat, Jean-Luc preached. He spoke to whoever had the inclination to listen about all he had written down and much more. He spoke about the great finger from beyond that had found Colmar a blemish on the face of the earth, deserving of destruction. He posited to his growing congregation that – considering it was what seemed to be a giant human finger that descended – reality was like a cosmic set of matryoshka dolls, with bigger and smaller versions of existence going off in both directions from their own, interacting rarely and providentially with each other, and that they were by no means the center. He failed to think big enough. Big enough, in this instance, being small enough, because that which he was calling God was the finger of a girl about his age in Indianapolis, Indiana.

As people continued to listen, Jean-Luc continued to create. From whole cloth, Jean-Luc created a new religion that suited him and the situation in which he found himself, and it felt fantastic. Like a maddened chef, he spiced and seasoned with abandon, adding and appropriating ingredients from a spectrum of sources. He let his religion grow into a philosophical Frankenstein's monster of his own liking, and the crowds around him continued to grow.

Eventually, they began to build. With wood brought in from neighboring towns, they started to erect an actual church edifice. Jean-Luc decided that his work there was done and that it was time for him to go out from that place. While the congregation continued to build, Jean-Luc set out on his undusted boots to spread the good news.

CHAPTER 9:

MAPS AREN'T MAGIC

DAMIEN GATHERED THE REST of the crew at the apartment later that afternoon. He prefaced his presentation with the understatement of the century: "Now, this is going to sound crazy."

He recounted to the group the events of the last few days: the fermented, inebriating rainstorm in New Orleans and the finger of god that destroyed part of France. He did so in the manner of a newscaster. These were the facts, and he would share them before he presented his and Madeleine's hypothesis.

"End of times," they said, half joking, half musing. He asked Madeleine if she wanted to take it from where he had left off. She did not. He explained that the evening before, Madeleine had pressed her finger against the dot marked Colmar on the map. Solemnity took the group for a brief second as each of their minds put two and two together and then scanned through a Rolodex of preset responses, none of which seemed appropriate for what they just heard. He continued to explain that the night of the event in New Orleans, they had been partying and that beer had been tossed around. It would be completely plausible to assume that some had found its way to the map, though it did seem unlikely.

"Maddie believes that her finger may have destroyed the city of Colmar through the map and that we may have poured beer over New Orleans during our party. And I'm starting to wonder if she's right. It does seem awfully, preposterously coincidental."

Chester and Arch, in utter incredulity, parried with a barrage of expletives and jokes. Their bravado once again astounded Damien, who thought on all the times Arch had shared a deeper self and insecurity with him, and Damien wondered if there was any confidence to him at all. He considered the possibility that swagger was nothing but well-pointed, finely tuned anxiety. They ran their mouths, flinging a flurry so thick that it would be impossible to see any fear hiding behind it. Was charisma just a meticulously sculpted and placed shield of refurbished anxiety? Was there nothing more than anxiety manifested in different ways? His skin felt tight. He considered the possibility that it was because he did not talk as much as they did. His anxiety was not being released in rambling. Erin and Peter sat quietly, entertaining the idea of a fantastical voodoo map capable of affecting the entire world.

"Why are we even talking about this? It's impossible."

"Look at the facts."

"There are no facts."

"Colmar is gone. That is a fact."

"Magic maps don't exist, dude."

Voices were rising.

"This is ridiculous. I'll touch it right now." Arch stood up on the couch where he was sitting and raised a flat palm to the map as a chorus of protests rang through the room. One voice seemed to bellow above the rest, deeper, and with weight.

"Don't," rang from Damien's mouth past a snarl and a frown. It was a look of strength and sincerity. Arch's hand hovered, and he stared sternly at Damien.

"If we're right," Damien said in a calm, controlled voice, "and you touch that map, you'll destroy a good portion of the entire world. Think about that. If we're right, you'll be committing genocide, you idiot. In one second, you'll commit genocide – probably be the biggest genocide the world has ever seen and you'll be responsible for it. Arch, we can't treat this how you normally treat things. We can't gamble on this. We need to find out another way."

Arch stood and stared at Damien, shoulders rising and falling, nostrils flaring ever so slightly, eyes unblinking, gears turning. "Rabbits love gambling," Arch said in another strangely calm voice, referencing again the billboard off I-465 that Chester and he had jested on just two nights before. No one laughed or smiled. He said, "Okay," and sat back down.

When met with something as philosophically challenging as this, different people's different worldviews react in a myriad of different ways. Some reject, solidifying their worldview; some accept and are still solidified; some crumble; some transcend and include. The whole spectrum of reactions was represented in the apartment that day.

After a good amount of arguing and tense conversation, it was decided that they needed to find out if this was actually happening. (Probably wise.) Peter glanced over his shoulder at the map hanging behind him and shuddered a bit, hoping no one saw.

"We can't just touch it," said Peter and shuddered again. Erin felt it that time. "How can we find out if we …" He trailed off as he tried to figure out how to even talk about something so fantastical. "If we have a voodoo map. … We shouldn't just touch it outright. Let's see if getting close to it makes something happen first. Then, maybe, we touch it. Everything we've done to it so far, assuming this is true and the map is magic, has had huge repercussions here in the real world. Anything else we do, we need to do somewhere that there's room for error. Maybe we could do something to a lake or body of water." The whole speech felt ridiculous as it rolled off his tongue.

After a bit more deliberation, undertaken much more calmly, probably due to Peter's levelheaded interjection, they started to form a plan. Damien came up with it when it all came down to it, but they truly did work in unison. Every battalion needed a vanguard, and though it was usually one of the discursive duo, occasionally Damien assumed the position. Damien explained his plan.

One member of the group would hover a toothpick over Lake Michigan just off the Indiana shoreline. The rest of them would drive out to the Indiana Dunes where the lake – and presumably, the tip of the toothpick – could be seen from the shore. They were afraid to touch anywhere, even lightly, holding to the assumption that even the smallest amount of direct contact would have devastating repercussions there on terra firma. But with a toothpick and a lake, they were hoping the smallest amount of contact possible could be made. The hope was that the tip of the toothpick would be visible once it got within a certain distance of the map, and they would not have to touch the map at all.

They decided that Chester and Arch would stay back to hover the toothpick and the other four would take the trip to Northwest Indiana, mostly because neither Chester nor Arch bought into the paranoia much, or at least acted like they did not, and they said they did not want to waste any money on gas, snacks, cigarettes.

"It's a map," they kept saying.

"Maps aren't magic," they kept saying.

Peter shuddered.

CHAPTER 10:

GIVETH // TAKETH

THE NEXT MORNING, AS the Ripple Six stepped into the outside world, there was a significant chill in the air. Winter weather can be so ominous. It awakens the senses and alerts the mind, and if there is anything mysterious in the air, it becomes doubly so with the cold. Like a television studio audience kept in a sixty-degree climate to ensure hearty responses and no sleepers, the Six were immediately brought into the pinnacle of awareness when they stepped outside, ready to respond to what the day had to offer.

Damien, Madeleine, Erin, and Peter threw backpacks full of varying amounts of snacks, books, clothes, and other accoutrements into Madeleine's 2007 Honda Civic and set out for the lake. Before leaving, Damien walked up to Arch and pressed his palms against both sides of Arch's head, holding the stoner's head gingerly, like one would hold a touchy explosive.

"Do not screw around today. If this is really happening and you make a mistake, it will be extremely not good. All I'm saying is that I've never seen Madeleine like this before."

"I got it, man," Arch responded with his usual, unbridled level of well-sculpted and well-pointed anxiety.

Damien nodded and walked toward the car. Before getting in, he looked over his shoulder and said, "Don't smoke too much," and got in the back seat with Peter.

Madeleine put the car in drive, and they were off. The air in the car was thick, not entirely because of Damien's excessive cigarette smoking, but because they were all uncertain about what they were going to find. They were all afraid and a little excited that they might discover that they were right about the map. Damien thought about whether there was a word for that emotion. Peter counted the puffs Damien took on his cigarettes. Madeleine focused on the road. Erin wondered what everyone else was thinking about.

Erin was also sitting in the passenger seat playing disc jockey. She played a song by an instrumental band that Madeleine had shown her in college. Damien recognized it because he had been the one who showed them to Madeleine in the first place.

Sitting in the back seat with Peter, Damien began to think about what he could do if they found out the map gave him godlike control over all of humanity. Damien giveth, and Damien taketh away? It did not sound right. The biggest decisions he had to make on a daily basis were what he would eat, what coffee shop he would play, and how tight to hug his girlfriend. He would have so much control if it was true. He thought about the role he would play. He was thinking about himself too much. Or was he? This was something he would have to think about.

Peter smelled the rich exhaust from the end of Damien's cigarette and wanted one badly. Sometimes it was hard for Peter to find contentment between big events, and cigarettes had always helped him pass that time. Cigarettes didn't make the line from event A to event B any shorter, but they seemed to make the line dance a little. They made the time in between feel like a little party. But they borrowed time from the ends of the line. That energy had to come from somewhere. So was he willing to trade a few minutes from the end of his life for the line to dance a bit now?

This time between events would be a little more enjoyable, but he would get to experience fewer events because his time on Earth would be a little bit shorter. He would take from the number of his days to give to the day he was currently living. Peter giveth, and Peter taketh away. *This is what we will have to consider if the map is what we think it is,* he thought. *With everything we give, we will take something away. We will need to do the math and make calculated decisions.* He decided against smoking once again in that moment.

Erin carefully chose a new song, this time deciding on a pop song. She, in the role of disc jockey, felt self-importance. She felt control over the mood in the car, though this control was not actually hers. They listened to a young pop star sing about the search for transcendence of thought, fear, and pain in a party scene. Erin had to get everyone's mind away from the task at hand. When the song came to an end, she switched to an Irish punk band and looked in the rearview mirror. Damien had begun to nod his head to the beat. She internalized this and felt she had done a good job. She gave herself a mental pat on the back. *This is what we have to do with the map. We can make the world dance. Could we play music to the map? Could we make everyone forget about pain and anxiety? Should we forget about pain and anxiety, even for a moment?* There was a lot to consider, and she was in control. Erin giveth, and Erin taketh away.

Madeleine's mind continued to race. It hadn't stopped racing since the day before. She did not want this power. Driving the car was more power than she particularly wanted. She wished she was taking pictures. But then she thought about that word: *taking.* When she took pictures, what was she doing? She was immortalizing a moment by taking its own visage from it. Was her photography a form of theft? Was she stealing from her subjects? No, of course not. She was giving them that moment forever. She was compounding the moment by creating an infinite number of moments upon it. A new moment was created every single time someone looked at one of her photos. So by taking, she was giving. Madeleine giveth, and Madeleine taketh away. *In every action*, she thought, *there is gift and theft*. She just had to weigh out whether the cost was worth the benefit.

The four barreled up I-65 for about an hour and a half, thinking about gift and theft, gain and loss, before Madeleine decided that she had to pee. They stopped at a Circle K for a minute, and Damien volunteered to drive the rest of the way.

When they got back in the car, Madeleine got her camera and began snapping a few photos of her friends. Erin and Peter feigned smiles, but Damien did not really try. He looked at her with severity in his eyes, but he always did this. She loved him for his severity. She leaned in close and kissed his shoulder and then snapped a photo of his hands on the steering wheel. His knuckles were white. He was gripping it tight so as to feel every inch of the road and movement of the vehicle, that way he had control. If he was in control, things could not go wrong. Madeleine went on compounding moments, and Erin and Peter sang the songs that Erin played over the speakers.

The Indiana Dunes were quickly approaching.

CHAPTER 11:

MAUNDY

THEY GOT OUT OF the car at a place often visited for the sake of celebration. Today, the purpose of the place was somber experimentation. The sun was not quite directly overhead. It shone almost completely uninhibited by clouds, but little to no heat reached them. Peter had counted only twenty-three clouds in the sky. They were not very big either. The grass on the shore of Lake Michigan seemed to whisper in the frigid wind, beckoning them, "Come and see." They closed the doors to the sedan and started walking toward the shore.

Damien removed his phone from his pocket as they got closer and called Arch. "Hello?" sang the voice through the phone.

"Hey, man," Damien replied. "We're here. Are you ready?" The situation called for brevity in his opinion.

"I don't know how anyone could ever be ready," said Arch, and then he breathed quickly, forcefully, and loudly out his nose, almost like he was about to muster a laugh then realized in a micromoment that no laugh belonged there and sequestered the airflow to his nose.

"Alright," said Damien, "let's do it." The four stopped on the beach a good distance from the ebb and flow of the tide.

"Hold on."

Arch grabbed the toothpick he had prepared for the occasion, put the phone on speaker, and placed it on the back of the couch.

The four beachgoers lined up from left to right in this order: Peter, Damien, Madeleine, Erin, with Erin and Peter about a foot behind the other two, forming an unintended wedge, ready for battle. They planted their feet in the sand. Damien stood strong a few inches in front of Madeleine. He was the vanguard again, the tip of the spear. He placed the arm not holding the phone behind his back.

"How close should I get it to the shore where you guys are?" he asked.

"Give it some space," spoke Damien. This may not have been the right answer, but he spoke quickly, eagerly desiring the answer to the bigger question at hand. It loomed over him and shaded him in uncertainty. "Not too much space though." It was time to find out.

"Okay, tell me when you see it."

Arch slowly started pushing the toothpick toward the tiny Lake Michigan before him. His brow furrowed. He licked his lips and set his jaw.

"Focus, Arch," he told himself. He pushed it farther forward with care and intention, like he was building a house of cards or a model ship in a bottle. He started to think about playing Operation as a kid. He got to about two inches from the map and paused.

"Can you see it?" he asked.

"No, not yet," replied Damien.

He pushed his hand a few more centimeters forward, and his hand gave a tremor. "Now?"

"No."

A centimeter more. "Now?"

"No."

A centimeter more. "Now?"

"No."

A centimeter. "Now?"

"No."

A centimeter. "Now?"

"No."

A centimeter more.

Not much changed in the way of inflection throughout the interaction. Arch was a little less than an inch from the blue ink upon the map, and his hand was shaking more and more with each passing second.

"Now?" he asked.

"Negatory," Damien replied.

"I honestly cannot get much closer," Arch said with a hint of exasperation in his tone. "I think I'm going to have to touch it."

Damien's heart flipped over, and for some reason the first line of "Juicy" by Biggie Smalls popped into his head and he felt a hope that it was true. He pinched himself mentally and hoped that it was all a dream. He did not wake up.

"Alright. Do it. I'll let you know when I see something."

Five centimeters away. Four centimeters away. Three centimeters away.

"Nothing yet. Nothing yet. Nothing yet."

Two centimeters.

"Nothing yet. Nothing …"

One.

"Nothing."

Touchdown.

In that moment, a lot happened. Arch gently pressed the tip of the toothpick to the map and felt a bolt of electricity run up his arm. He felt a shudder, a shake, a chill all at once. His eyes widened, and his teeth met in his mouth. A gentle breeze seemed to run outward from the wall and tickle his face and ears.

One hundred and fifty miles away, at the Indiana Dunes, the eyes of the few at the beach that day – the brave, the curious – were gifted with a great and unbelievable vision. Stupefied, they looked on in horror and excitement as the sky about two hundred feet up began to rift and give birth to a gigantic birch point. A wave of force rippled outward in all directions and hit those on the beach like a powerful gust of wind. Erin and Peter both reeled backwards a bit. Damien stayed planted, unblinking and mortified as his hair whipped a bit around him in the blast.

"Maps aren't magic," Madeleine whimpered.

"I see it," Damien said into the phone.

The massive, pointed piece of birch emerged fully from the rift and grew conically in all directions. It continued to lower as Arch kept it pressed against the paint, and it quickly reached the water. As it touched the surface, a large splash erupted into the air, and a sound that the four had only heard in movies reached their ears. It was the sound of something colossal crashing into a body of water. The displaced water around the toothpick began to rise and subsequently fall as it was pushed outward, creating what seemed to be a pretty substantial wave from the shore. These aquatic echoes moved outward in all directions, pushing toward the four.

It occurred to Damien that this was proof of the fact that the world could truly be impacted by the map. Things could be moved, affected, disrupted, destroyed by his map. What was once yesterday's folly was now today's growing concern.

The waves – increased in the minds of the four on the shore by the fact that they should not be happening at all, according to their preexisting and now shattering paradigms – reached the shore in a much smaller state than the one in which they began. But still, the water pushed forward and toward the four. Their mouths hung agape as the water reached their shoes.

Peter and Madeleine both stepped back a few feet to avoid the wash, and Peter said, "Oh my God."

Erin and Damien did not move. Erin had removed her shoes when they stepped onto the beach to feel the sand between her toes, and quite a bit had accumulated there by now. She felt the icy Lake Michigan water wash over her feet a good twenty to thirty feet away from where the tide had previously been reaching and realized that the reason for this foot washing lay in her friends' apartment in Broad Ripple. The water washed the sand off her feet and back out across the beach, leaving her toes clean and white as the day she was born. She mentally wrestled with the fateful foot washing administered by a stoner nearly two hundred miles away.

Damien let the wash take him. He had not had a concise, definable, pursuable thought since the moment it registered that his map was magic. He just stood there through the series of supernatural events without allowing any inner dialogue or commentary. He let it all sink in. This was happening.

I am here now, he reminded himself. He owned a device with which he could literally control the world. He could make the world act in the way he wanted. He began to feel a weight and not just because his shoes were soaked by the wake.

As Damien stood there, the words began to form in his mind. They came quicker this time. Normally, they took their time as they became acquainted with each other in his verses. Now, in the wake, they were almost aggressive, reckless in the way they slammed together in the recesses of his mind.

The lonely ocean broken toasted by deific notion
The most impotent roasted bloke floats to coax the sky to open
We stood shored and roped at hope to see the coasted motion
How little do we know?

CHAPTER 12:

I AM BECOME PAN,

THE DESTROYER OF WORLDS

DAMIEN AWOKE IN WHAT first appeared to be a white space. But as his vision focused and his bearings gathered, it became apparent that *white* was hardly the word for it. A better descriptor would be *clear*. Damien saw no blemish, no deviation from purity. Safety washed over him like a cloak.

First, he looked down. Below him were two legs covered in thick, chestnut-colored fur, crossed in the Indian-style position. What a wonderful set of legs. He knew they were muscular despite the fur covering them. At the end of the legs were two cloven hooves, black, clean, and reflective.

Damien's eyes moved upward and noticed that the furry legs connected to a less furry, but still slightly so, well-fit torso. To each side of the torso was a thin, gangly arm ending in furry, nearly human hands, held palms upward, with the tips of the thumbs and pointer fingers of each individual hand pressed together. His eyes continued to climb the frame. His eyes climbed the frame until they could not climb any more, and it occurred to him that the furry legs, the cloven hooves, the toned, fuzzy stomach, the thin, muscled arms, the meditatively positioned hands were all his.

He wiggled his fingers, and they did. He flexed his stomach, and it did. He moved his legs a bit, and they did. He separated his pressed fingers and stretched them straight, bringing his arms upward toward his face. Before he reached his chin, he felt thin, wispy hairs hanging in a goatee from himself and gave it a stroke. He followed the goatee up to his chin and then his cheeks and lips. They felt like his cheeks and lips – finally, something was as he remembered. The sides of his face bore thick sideburns, and atop his head was a curled tuft of thick hair. From that hair, on each side of the top of his head, he felt something hard emerging from – but still attached to – his scalp. His hands traversed the protrusions. He felt thick rods with distinct fluting. He followed them to their tips, and they spiraled and bent and curved the whole way up. He had horns.

After the initial shock of his incredible transformation into what seemed to be some sort of goat had worn off, he noticed a few more specific things about his surroundings. Orbiting him, inexplicably, were dozens of clean, shining glass orbs, each containing something different. In one, there was nothing but stars. In another, he saw a herd of deer running through a field of tall, beige grass. One orb seemed to hold nothing but water. Another seemed to hold nothing but fire. Many of them seemed to hold scenes of nature and elements, but not all of them. His eyes continued to scan the orbs until they landed on one that contained, he noticed, the face of his friend Arch. The next one he saw held the face of Erin. Then he found one with Peter's, in another Chester's, and lastly, one orbiting sphere held the face of his love, Madeleine.

Damien's arms and hands seemed to have automatically returned to their prayerful position at his sides after examining his face and horns. His arms were once again horizontal with palms facing upward, thumbs and pointers pressed together firmly.

He felt connected to the orbs. He felt each of their rotations in his heart and knew exactly where each one was whether he was looking at it or not. He thought to himself that he would like for them to rotate slower so that he could look at them closer. Immediately and gracefully, they slowed their rotation.

Strange, he thought.

Allowing them to return to their original speed, he looked at the one containing water, and with the pinky, ring, and middle fingers on his right hand, he beckoned it toward himself. It complied, floating slowly toward him and then hovering in front of his face. Looking inside he saw vast, swirling oceans and tempestuous waves. He motioned the orb away from him, and it returned to its place in the rotation.

He began playing with the orbs. He had them spin in reverse. He had them swim past each other and out of rotation. Waving his arms around, the orbs danced all throughout the clear space. When he threw his arm to the left, the orb he was focusing on followed. He had one containing Peter fly to his pointer finger and spin on the tip of it like a basketball. The orbs were at his beck and call, flying anywhere he wanted them to go. They flew past his head at a close but controlled distance. They flew past each other in the same fashion. He waved his arms around like a deranged orchestra conductor. He started to let them graze each other a little.

When this happened, his eyes went red and so did the clear, white space he was in. A loud, cacophonous hum filled the air, and the orbs picked up their speed. First, he threw his arms forward, and the orbs flew at a breakneck speed away from him and into the vast, unknown space ahead. Then he powerfully and violently pulled his arms back to his sides and closed his fists. As he did, the orbs flew toward him even faster and past him. They spun around him again.

He pictured the fire orb and the water orb and stuck his arms straight out to his sides, his fingers stretched and his palms facing forward, and then he brought them quickly to the space in front of him, clapping his hands loudly together. When this happened, the fire orb and the water orb slammed together and exploded, and the red hue of the space turned darker. He did this with orb after orb until only his friends were left, so he slammed his friends together. First, he slammed Chester and Arch. When he did this, he hurt. He wanted to be done with the performance but did not know how to be done. Then he slammed Peter and Erin and felt the same feeling.

The only orb remaining was Madeleine. He played with her for a bit. She flew past him and around him and far from him and then near. A dark, thick, bloodred surrounded him and filled his eyes. He brought her toward himself and held her firmly between his furry, nearly human hands. Then he began to push. Every fiber of his being said no, but still he pushed. Her beautiful, perfect orb began to squeeze and bend. His essence screamed for release, but still he pushed. He squeezed her orb with little to no exertion. It was so easy. He squeezed until she was a flat disc between his palms and screamed. He prayed not to do what he was about to do. He dug his nails into the flattened Madeleine orb and pulled it apart. He threw the two halves of the orb away from each other in opposite directions, still screaming, and felt his entire world destroyed at his own hands.

Damien awoke covered in sweat, screaming, "Let me out!" Madeleine shot up, startled but still in one piece, from where she had been lying at his side.

CHAPTER 14:

PRIMUM NON NOCERE

FOR THREE DAYS, NOBODY touched the map, but they talked and thought about nothing else. Conversation about next steps went on through those few days. They discussed giving it to the police, but unfortunately, they – specifically Madeleine – were responsible for a certain number of deaths. Afraid that she would be tried for a mass murder, they decided against turning the map over immediately. She did not know that she was destroying a town and its surrounding areas by pointing out a dream destination to her boyfriend, but the fact stood that she did destroy a town and its surrounding areas.

While a power as great as Damien's map had immense potential for good, it could not be forgotten that the map also gave them an unfathomable capacity for destruction, so they decided on a pact. They would not use the map for evil, if they used it at all. That, to all of them, seemed to be the necessary ingredient for success: the pursuit of good. Even though good and evil were a bit elusive in identification sometimes, they would only pursue what appeared to be good.

They also recognized that they were all dumb, they were all human, and they occasionally had thoughts they should not have, desires they should not have, and a periodic proclivity for hate. They would need to keep this in consideration. Given that occasional appetite for destruction and the map at their fingertips, they recognized that the potentiality and probability of tragedy were amplified. Damien fought the urge to quote Uncle Ben from Spiderman and say, "With great power comes great responsibility." Chester fought no such urge, and the group chuckled a bit. It was good to laugh.

They needed some words to live and die by. They needed something all-encompassing and powerful. They decided on a phrase that Peter proposed, *primum non nocere*, as their credo and mantra in possession and usage of the map going forward. Peter's mother was a doctor, and when he was growing up, she had told him about the expression. When she started medical school, she and her peers were taught this as a fundamental principle of healthcare.

Primum non nocere.

First, do no harm.

Peter explained that his mother had taught him that sometimes it was better to do nothing than to do something that could potentially be harmful. If the decision was either to act and risk harm or not to act, a person should land on not acting most of the time. There would be contention. There was no way to completely know the results of an action, but in the interest of *primum non nocere*, any decision they made with the map should, in theory, cause no harm.

Any decision will always have collateral, especially decisions of this magnitude. The four who took the trip to the Indiana Dunes were really starting to consider this. When someone gives something, they take something else away. When they give something up, something else is lost. When something is decided upon, something else is decided against. But in the pursuit of only help, harm could be minimalized in the grand scheme. It was do something entirely good or do nothing at all.

Damien thought they were naïve thinking it would be possible to do exclusive good or to do nothing on such a grand scale, or any scale at all. When something is given, something is taken. When something is found, something is lost. When something is decided, something else is decided against. If they were to help someone, they were withholding help from someone else. That could be considered a form of harm. When Peter pointed out that they were probably overthinking it, Damien continued to worry. There was going to be harm. "The best-laid schemes of mice and men often go awry," flashed across his mind. Then he thought of Chester and Arch. They had anxiety, but they aimed it and acted. He could do this too. They would have to act. The decision was in their hands.

Primum non nocere is what they decided upon, deciding against something else, hoping that they would be able to do good.

CHAPTER 15:

ENCOURAGEMENTS FOR ERIN

"OKAY, SO WE WANT to help people. How?" asked Madeleine poignantly and fearfully. This was a good question. What could they do with the device that would only help people and avoid hurt entirely?

Chester and Arch had a couple ideas to pitch, speaking up first, once again, with haste and reckless abandon. Chester thought it would be fun to mess with people. They could find a way to hover a large disc, emulating a spaceship. It would be like a modern-era, supernatural version of the 1938 radio broadcast of *The War of the Worlds*, but this would cause much more panic than the original. He was promptly reminded that they were going to try not to cause any harm and that fear and panic were extremely harmful. He jokingly argued that it was a harmless prank and that fear could be used as a tool to keep people in check. He also argued that for the "believers" in the world, their entire life would be made. "It's very important for people to believe in things beyond themselves," he said with a snicker and a wry smile.

Arch's brilliant next suggestion was to push something riveted into the map. Then they could travel to the location where it touched down and try to climb it. If they made it all the way to the top where it emerged into the world through a hole in the sky, they could travel through the portal and, according to his theory, climb through the map into their very own apartment. This idea was probably harmless but not very productive. Plus, it could lead to them being discovered as the owners of the map. Both of these cockamamie ideas were negated with haste. It was mind-boggling to most of the group how cavalier they were both being. They had such violent nonchalance, it seemed sometimes as if they were caricatures of real people. It felt like they were nothing more than an archetype in a novel, existing just to prove a point.

Damien thought briefly about the man with the bullhorn they had seen in Broad Ripple and what might happen if the map fell into the hands of a person with so much condemnation in his heart. He saw people running and screaming under a darkened sky, their bodies wreathed in flames. The voice of the man echoed in his mind once again. "Forevermore," it said and said again.

Peter had the idea of speaking into the map, which might act as a PA system, and they could broadcast messages from "God" to the entire world. They would only speak messages of peace, love, and harmony: "Love each other," "Give to the poor," "Do not fear those of other races." If they said things like this, people would believe God was commanding them to be better people, and they would oblige. Damien pointed out that God already commanded people to do this in the Bible, and everyone still sucked. Peter argued that this would change things. Hearing a voice from the heavens would really impact people. It would be a modern-day reminder of the commands of old. It would make God real. Whether God was real or not, it would make people believe again that He was, and belief is just as powerful as fact. Chester thought they should say, "Greetings, earthlings," into the map.

This being the first good, actionable idea the group had to date, they decided to test it out. Peter would have to speak since it was his thought baby, and on top of that, the gang considered him to be the most holy of them with his faith and superstition. Madeleine said she wanted to stay up in the apartment with Peter as he spoke, and everyone else stepped out front of the apartment and turned their eyes upwards. Once they were outside, Damien called Madeleine and told her they were ready. She relayed the information to Peter.

Peter leaned toward the magic map hanging on the wall in front of him. He squinted a little as he felt a wave of heat radiate off it. He could not be sure whether his psyche created waves of force emanating from the instrument of power or if real energy was coming from the item. He brought his mouth into the space above where Indiana was marked on the map, within a foot of the surface, and said, "Hello." His voice quivered and crackled, and he hardly croaked it out. "Hello?" he said again.

"Anything?" whispered Madeleine into the phone.

"Well, I'm not hearing anything out of the ordinary," Damien replied. "Maybe get a little closer."

"A little closer," she whispered to Peter.

He obliged and leaned in closer, which he hated, and he began to tremble a bit. One errant movement and his nose could bump the map and cause an earthquake, another crushing, a horrible flood. His mind reeled with horrible possibilities. His mouth was now within a couple inches of the surface.

"Hello," he said a bit louder this time. "Testing. One, two, three."

His eyes darted a bit. He felt embarrassed speaking into the map like a microphone, which felt a bit foolish, especially in front of Madeleine.

"Anything?"

"Nothing."

No voice of God rang out across Indianapolis that afternoon. No heavenly hello rattled the eardrums of the Ripple Six. It seemed that, just as God himself seemed to do most often in the modern era – if there was a God at all – they would need to communicate with the mortals of earth by acting, not speaking.

They reconvened in the apartment, and all gave Peter pats on the back, hugs, and a volley of "Good idea, man."

"Are you okay?" Madeleine asked him, and he sheepishly nodded yes. He was a bit disappointed that his plan had fallen through, but it was good to know more about the map than they did before. He sat down on the end of the couch, his hands clasped between his thighs, his knees pressed tightly together, the ends of his feet pointed inward. He squeezed his hands tight with his thighs and took a deep breath. It truly was a jarring experiment, but he felt relieved that he caused neither harm nor good.

Thank God I'm not God, he thought almost subconsciously, unintentionally, as if the words flashed across his mind like a cerebral marquee.

Arch looked across the room at sweet Erin's smooth, expressionless face. Beautiful and blank, it waited for prompting on what to do next. She seemed good because she was nothing. She was he and all of them, and they were good so she was too. He remembered stories of her Christian good-doing in her past.

"Erin, didn't you spend some time doing mission work back in the day?"

With that inspiration from Arch, the neurons began firing in her sweet, simple mind, and her face came to life. A brightness came to her otherwise dull eyes, and where a pleasantly closed, emotionless mouth usually sat, a smile crested. She recalled a summer she spent in Africa with YWAM when she was in high school and proposed they help someone there. There was severe financial need, and Africa had some of the most food- and water-insecure places on Earth. Plus, there were wide-open spaces where she assumed it would be safe to drop something into the map. The heads of the Ripple Six nodded approvingly at her good idea.

"We know that a finger and a toothpick went into the map and then were pulled out. If we drop something, I imagine it would stay." Erin was being a bit presumptuous to have been assuming so much, especially with something with such potential, but she was human and she was bound to make mistakes with the map.

As conversations about specifics – the where, the what, and the how – began, Madeleine asked if anyone wanted coffee. There was a resounding "yes," and she walked to the kitchen. A quick google led by Chester revealed that the country of Burundi was a prime candidate for their beneficence. It was rated poorest and most food insecure on a few separate lists and had wide-open spaces where a gift could be dropped. Over half the country lived below the poverty line. It had also recently come out of thirteen years of civil war.

Next, they needed to decide what they would give to the poor people of Burundi. Madeleine returned with various mugs filled with cheap, Folgers breakfast blend coffee made in a stained, old coffee pot. Damien always insisted that the stains added to the flavor. She heard his voice in her head as she was making it. The mugs had a variety of different logos, phrases, and pictures printed on them. One mug had a picture of Spiderman, along with onomatopoeic words like "Bang!" "Thwip!" and "Slam!" Another mug had a dinosaur on it that read, "All my friends are dead." Another mug was solid grey and bore a faded emblem of something now unrecognizable. It had probably faded after many trips through the dishwasher. Yet another mug was a clean, white mug with snoopy sleeping on his doghouse on one side.

Chester said, "Yes," as he was handed a large, brown mug that said in big, white block letters, "Coffee makes me poop." He took a sip from the crass, brown mug and returned his attention to the Wikipedia page for Burundi glowing in front of him. He prepared to make a decision of equal caliber to one made by a world leader while holding a mug that read, "Coffee makes me poop."

"Things get bigger when they go in the map," said Damien, "so whatever we drop needs to be incredibly small."

"We could drop food. Let's roll up some bread, ham, and cheese into a little ball and drop that. It would feed Africa forever," said Arch.

"It would not feed Africa forever. It would go bad," said Damien.

"But I want to see a big sandwich ball," said Arch, dejected.

Damien chuckled. "That would be gold."

Erin's mind once again came to life. The electricity raced from synapse to synapse, and smoke began to pour from her ears. At Damien's verbal cue, she became inspired. Now, two for two, Erin remembered a souvenir box of gold dust that she had gotten on a family vacation to Juneau, Alaska, as a child and brought it up to the group. It was perfect. A small fleck of pure gold could be dropped into the map using a pair of tweezers. It would grow in size and turn Burundi immediately into an extremely wealthy country. It was decided as the best course of action. Erin grabbed her jacket and ran home to get her little box of gold. Damien volunteered to walk to the pharmacy for a pair of tweezers.

CHAPTER 16:

DAMIEN THINKS

THROUGH THINGS

DAMIEN STEPPED OUT OF his apartment and instinctively removed a light-blue packet of American Spirit cigarettes from his jacket pocket. He pulled one of the remaining cigarettes from the pack and placed it between his lips. From the same pocket he removed a lighter that had a pickle on it and lit the cigarette. It was travel time.

He started walking toward the CVS on the corner three blocks south of his apartment and felt relaxed. He and his friends were a part of the biggest event in human history, to his knowledge, and they were not doing too badly of a job. They were being careful, intentional, and smart about the whole affair. A betting man would have probably placed his money on them all spiraling into panic by now and jumping out a window.

No one had ever had power like this before as far as he knew, except God, if God ever existed. There was no way to be sure that God existed. He was sure that Damien existed though. Actually, he was pretty sure that he existed. Actually, he could not be sure that he existed at all. He continued to walk down the street confidently unsure that he was there at all, believing it wise to always doubt himself. So he went down the street contradicting every thought that sprang to mind, making progress geographically, running circles philosophically. He diagnosed foolishness on the theists and solipsists alike and continued on his merry way.

One, two, three
Keep your mind from certainty
Those concrete shoes will carry you
To bed in a cerebral sea

Four, five, six
No thought will ever stick
Best let them slide and then subside
And form a new one quick

Seven, eight, nine
It all will fade in time
It starts to fade the day it's made
So let your darlings die

How boring he found it to define anything at all in those days. Definition was limitation. To define something would be to limit its growth and, in turn, limit the growth of the observer who no longer had anything to learn about the thing observed. Once something was prescribed to be something, it could no longer act outside its description or it would cease to be. How boring it was to define his own being. How boring it was to define God. How boring it was to define poetry, politics, and maps filled with magic.

Damien walked past a group of middle schoolers in puffy jackets who seemed to be on a field trip. He assumed they were going to the theatre around the corner to see a troupe of middle-aged, hobbyist actors put on a lackluster rendition of *Romeo and Juliet*, leaving completed lines and accurate accents to the professionals. He remembered a similar field trip that he went on to that same theatre when he was in eighth grade. He saw *Hamlet*.

He wondered if any of the students walking past him had even the foggiest idea of who he was or what he possessed. He wondered if they thought of him at all. Then he thought back to his own field trip and the hundreds of cars and pedestrians that passed him by that day and could not remember anything about any of them besides the fact that they existed, so he must not have considered them or wondered what sort of magic items they possessed. He took this to mean that none of the kids passing by him were thinking of him either.

"No one knows what I'm up to. How could they know?" But he did not know that they were thinking this. And he did not know that they did not know. Maybe one of those little down jackets on legs had telepathic abilities. Weird things seemed to be happening.

He thought of all the people walking around him, some with sinister intentions, some with the best. He did not know what they were up to. They did not know what he was up to. He thought back again to his field trip and the people that passed by him that day. One of the people he passed that day could have been walking to CVS to buy a pair of tweezers so that they could drop a speck of gold into an enchanted map and he would have been none the wiser. There was no way he could know whether he had thought about it at the time or not. He suddenly felt a little less unique, a little less empowered. He felt connected to the hypothetical person he supposedly passed when he was an eighth grader while he wore a down jacket who was doing something magical and important just like Damien, thinking that there was no one like him as he passed someone like him. He began to get lost in his mind, enamored with this feeling of sonder, a feeling that everyone else was just like him. As far as feelings go, it was both constructive and deconstructive, building him up in the way it tore him down.

In that moment, he began to feel completely unspectacular, and it excited him. It felt good to imagine that there had been other people like him, that there might be other people in his position. They must have done alright. He did not know that they existed. If they had messed up, he probably would have heard about it. Heroes are often forgotten by history. Villains find it hard to keep their names from the record. Maybe he would do a good job with this map after all. If there were others like him, and if there had always been others like him – even when he was in eighth grade – and the world had not been destroyed, maybe he would not destroy the world because he was not special, and he was not unique.

But there would be none like him, he suddenly thought with resolve. He would do things that no one else was able to do. He was free from the bonds of congealed belief systems. He would be able to make decisions with unprecedented diplomacy. He slipped into thinking himself unique again, forgetting the conclusions he had come to just moments before.

He picked up a pair of tweezers at the pharmacy, paying two dollars and ninety-nine cents for one of the most important purchases of all time. *If only the cashier knew what I was up to*, he thought. *Maybe they do*, he thought a moment after that. *How could they?* he thought just one second later. He left the store and headed back toward the apartment.

Damien walked and thought, traversing the cluttered corners of his mind for twenty-five minutes, and at the end of it, he had gotten nowhere in his thinking and decided on nothing. He had traveled six blocks geographically and returned to the same place from which he departed at the beginning of his journey. Philosophically, he had essentially done the same thing. Every time a thought started to form and firm, every time a shape was assembled in the mess of his mind, he pulled an operative string, and the shape loosened.

CHAPTER 17:

MARK

ARCH, IN HEADLESS HEDONISM, packed a bowl as soon as Damien left the apartment. Chester followed the lead of his fearless captain and addressed the other components to their insignificance-slaying ritual. He assuredly removed an eponymous rap record from its paper sleeve and placed it decidedly upon the turntable. He found purchase for the needle along the record's edge and turned the player on. The record was entirely apropos for the personalities of the two young men. The two rappers that comprised the group were quick in wit and word. They were violent. They were hasty. They talked braggadocious circles around the minds of their listeners and assumedly had the life experience to back it up. They were loquacious. But they were also the kind of people you wanted by your side when the rubber hit the road.

Next, Chester addressed the Xbox, finding Mass Effect in the machine, deeming it worthy, and returning to the couch next to Arch, who released an inaugural plume of smoke into the air and handed the piece to Chester. The smoke swirled and danced in the few rays of sun allowed by the blinds.

Peter and Madeleine felt the time inappropriate for such behavior and adjourned to the kitchen. Madeleine put on another pot of coffee, and Peter adjusted magnets on the refrigerator, simply passing time.

"Do you think the map has been used before?" he asked her.

"What do you mean?"

"Well, I can't imagine we're the first ones to ever have this in our hands. I wonder if anyone else has ever figured out what it does."

"I mean, it does seem old," Madeleine responded. "I can't remember anything like what's happened happening before we had the map, but I guess it's completely possible. There have been miracles, unexplainable things like UFOs that have been seen by people in the past. That could have been the map. Or something else ... Any number of things like this could exist. It took this long for this thing to surface. Do you think there are more or just this?"

"I don't know but I still feel like I'm about to wake up," Peter said, still moving magnets.

Some time passed, and Damien returned from his excursion and was greeted by a barrage of sights, smells, and sounds as he reentered the domicile. A ship flew through space on the television. A salvo of hypersexual, hyperaggressive, but incomparably clever lyrics cascaded from the record player. A usually friendly smell hung in the air. Arch was bloviating on the couch about how the Mass Effect series got everything right. It looked like any other day, which it was or was not.

Damien looked at them disapprovingly and asked, "How's your day going?"

"Quickly toward the night. You?" Arch responded without hesitation, eyes fixed firmly on the screen.

Damien shook his head, walked over, and turned off the television.

"What the heck, dude?" Arch asked.

Damien walked into the kitchen. As he caught the attention of Peter and Madeleine, he threw his thumb over his shoulder in the direction of Chester and Arch and shook his head again.

"I know," said Peter.

Arch grabbed the remote and turned on the television.

Damien gingerly kissed Madeleine on the top of her head and grabbed the coffee pot. Peter looked down at his hands. "Has anyone heard from Erin?" Damien asked.

"No," Peter responded. "Hey, do you think this thing has been used before?"

"I like to think so. I can't imagine something this fragile and powerful could exist for as long as it seems to have existed and not have been used. It must have been created for some reason too. I would imagine whoever or whatever made it, made it for a purpose. Or they didn't. But they probably used it when it was made. I don't know. Things have happened throughout time that can't be fully explained."

"That's what I said," Madeleine replied.

"Whether it has been used or not used," Peter chimed in, "I cannot imagine anyone is truly worthy of this kind of power. Let's be so careful, guys."

Damien nodded.

Erin came back into the apartment quietly and calmly. She nearly whispered her hellos, and as she entered, she seemed to shake her head in disapproval at the sights, sounds, and smells of the group's jesters on the couch.

"I found the gold pieces," she said loudly enough that the people in the kitchen could hear, and they started walking into the main area. Arch took the cue and turned off the television and the record player.

"Are we doing this thing?" he said.

"It seems so," Damien quickly responded.

Erin had been carrying a weight in her chest ever since she left the apartment, and it bubbled up into her throat. "I can't drop it." She sent a quick glance toward Madeleine, who carried a knowing concern in her brow. "It's too much," she continued. "I know my hand would shake and I'm scared and—"

"I can drop it," Peter said.

It was decided that the map should be laid flat, so they cleared the coffee table and gently removed it from the wall. As they moved it to the table, the air around them seemed to shudder. It pushed in on their frames and sent a tingle up their spines.

Chester had found a seemingly barren area near the Monge Forest and Mount Heha, south of Bujumbura, a place likely to hold tribes of the Great Lakes Twa people in the country of Burundi. The Great Lakes Twa were a Pygmy people forgotten by industry and civilization, oppressed by those they should call brothers. Miles of hills and plains provided perfect terrain for the drop, and the Batwa should be there. If anyone needed a golden gift, they did. He and Peter took a minute finding exactly the same spot on the map, and he prepared for the drop.

Peter took the small phial with a few gold flakes in it and unscrewed the lid. The bottle bore a small label describing the significance of its contents, a label that would, in a few moments, be made inaccurate. This fleck would be no mere remnant of a gold rush. This would save a country. Peter took the tweezers into his right hand and looked up at his friends.

"If we do this," he began, "we will be making our first intentional mark on this Earth. Are we ready for that?"

Damien sat with his hands folded in front of him, almost prayerfully. He looked at his hands and spoke quietly, but with an unprecedented sense of authority and confidence. "We make a mark every time we take a breath on this Earth. There's no telling what sort of impact each inhalation and exhalation will make. Sometimes the mark is big, and sometimes it's small. Sometimes it's beneficial, and sometimes it's not. But we have to breathe.

And we have to act. All we can do is do and hope for the best. Drop it."
He still did not look up.

Peter had a bit of doubt and a bit of distrust in his heart, but he had not seen his friend like this before. There was an unprecedented confidence. Damien had a belief in action so strong that Peter was moved. Damien had never shown much belief in anything besides Madeleine and music. Peter raised an eyebrow at his friend, lowered it, and moved his gaze to the map again.

No one said a word as Peter dropped the speck into the map in the area marked "Burundi." It disappeared into the surface without a ripple. They had made their first intentional mark on an unsuspecting world using the map, hoping to do no harm.

CHAPTER 18:

JOVANIS,

IN FOUR PARTS

PART I

JOVANIS LIFTED HIS GLISTENING brow to a fiendish midafternoon sun and squinted. There was one cloud in the blue of the sky. He prayed to nothing in particular that it would position itself between him and his friend, his foe, that torturous orb of orange. Nothing happened. He looked down, spit in the soil, and wiped his brow. His dark skin was silhouetted against the vibrant blue of the African sky, making the sky appear bluer, making him appear darker. Earlier that day, he had been blessed enough to enjoy a cup of locally sourced Burundian coffee, and his jolt was starting to fade. But the chickens were fed, and the garden tended. It seemed he had nothing pressing to do for the rest of the day. Sounds of pottery being made emerged from a hut about twenty feet from him. It was pottery that no one would buy. It was pottery that would fail to feed them.

With his chores for the day finished, he took a big breath, went to the well, and filled a tin cup with warm water. He took a sip and was refreshed. He squinted and saw near him a friendly baobab tree with which he had spent many a sweltering afternoon. He leaned his rippling back against it and squinted into the sky again.

He looked around his village and saw a small group of women coming back from the river, pots full of water sitting atop their heads and stiff necks. He saw children running and wrestling, one crying against a hut. He saw a man smoking as he turned a bird above a fire, presumably for dinner. He saw another man practicing nocking an arrow and shooting it from a bow on the outskirts of the village, the arrow sailing into that infinite blue. He saw a group of six men sitting around another fire toward the middle of the village, already drunk and speaking loudly. He saw the typical hustle and bustle of his village that no one outside the village ever considered, or so he assumed, and he felt a little bit of contentment, a little bit of discontent. They did not have a lot, but they were Twa; they were first, and they were proud.

As he continued to sit and squint, he heard a sound that he usually did not. A violent tearing sound rang out across the plain, and the sky opened. Immediately, another orange orb emerged from the rift. It was closer than the sun but equally as bright. He flinched backwards and squinted more, trying not to look away. It glistened and began tearing straight downward toward the earth, and he became sure he had fallen asleep against the baobab. The shimmering orb fell rapidly from the rift in the sky in a path that passed directly in front of its brother, the first sun, and completely blocked it out for a brief moment. Jovanis felt the shade he had prayed for not five minutes before provided by an unimaginable source. A scream erupted from the village. The second sun continued to rocket through the sky toward the arid Burundian landscape about three miles northeast of his village by his mark. It got closer and closer until, for a brief moment, he could not see it any longer. The landscape obscured the second sun momentarily before the earth heaved. A cacophonous boom accompanied a violent shudder of the earth beneath him, and he was dumbfounded and did not wake up. Seconds passed, and a cloud of dust rocketed into the sky where the second sun had fallen. He shot to his feet and ran toward the center of the village.

Panicked tones filled the air as his people left their huts, ranting in Rundi and trying to find an explanation for the tremor moments before. Mothers tended to their wailing children and looked around with furrowed brows. Men and young boys alike were running and grabbing weapons instinctively. He saw the group of drunks again who had been sitting around the fire in inebriated bliss. They were tending to one of their friends who had seemingly fallen into the flames when the orb hit the earth. He started calling for the chief who emerged from his hut moments later, looking befuddled but driven. He was a good chief.

Jovanis explained to the chief the supernatural event he had witnessed just moments before. A crowd started to gather around them. "A second sun fell from a tear in the sky. It hit the earth not three miles northeast. We must go find it."

The chief frowned, named four men, "Roan, Emery, Christian, and Jovanis," and said, "Go."

Jovanis and the other three nodded knowingly and rushed to their own individual huts to grab supplies. Jovanis hustled about his small, dirty domicile and grabbed his bow, his spear, and his waterskin. He suddenly realized this was the only truly exciting thing that had ever happened to him. He left his hut and ran to the northeast edge of the village. The other three came just moments later.

The four set out at a pace of about five and a half minutes per mile toward the dust cloud that still lingered ominously above the presumed location of the second sun. Sweat dripped from their skin as they bounded over bushes and squinted in the sun. Thousands of years of Pygmy survival pumped through their veins. Jovanis felt it. *We are Twa. We are strong.* They began bounding up a hill, and as they crested it, the second sun came into sight.

The four men stopped dead in their tracks. There, in the basin before them, lay a shimmering, gilded rock standing over two hundred feet tall and two hundred feet wide. It sparkled in the sun. They squinted even more than usual, and Jovanis felt a chill run up his spine. Its surface was jagged and pockmarked. Jovanis had heard of this substance but had never seen it before. He looked at his compatriots, and they looked back at him. There, in Burundi, near a small village of the Batwa people, slightly clouded by dust, sat twenty stories of solid gold.

PART II

PETER LOOKED UP FROM his computer at his friends.

"Did you guys know a humpback whale's cry can be heard for up to twelve miles?"

PART III

THE SECOND SUN BURNED bright in Jovanis' mind. He and the rest of the scouting party had arrived back at the village just moments before. The mammoth, golden rock sat currently unattended as far as he knew. Sweat dripped from his brow.

One of Jovanis' compatriots had raced to the chief's hut immediately upon arriving, and Jovanis and the rest had started assembling everyone in the middle of the village. The people, chattering incessantly, understandably so, began to gather around. Chief Alain, a wise, wizened old man, approached the chattering crowd. He walked with a bit of a hunch. It was the hunch of a man who had carried countless, immeasurable weights upon his shoulders but had never stopped carrying, had never stopped walking, and had never stopped accepting something else to carry. He was the kind of man who would joke about his own fragility while weathering harrowing storms with aplomb.

"So, what do we have?" Alain said in Rundi. He looked calmly from man to man until one spoke. It was not Jovanis. Jovanis had looked intently at the chief when the chief looked at him, nodded, but did not speak. He figured someone else should explain the situation. He figured his gifts lay elsewhere.

A man named Roan, six inches shorter than Jovanis and slightly stockier, spoke up and explained to the chief that just northeast of the village, lying presumably unattended, were tons of what seemed to be solid gold. Alain made Roan repeat this word, "Gold."

In Rundi, whispers of "How can this be?" floated through the small crowd. Roan continued, insisting that he could not be sure that it was gold and that he doubted that it was gold at all. It had fallen from the sky after all. But it felt and looked like gold, impossible as that may be.

There was a silence as Chief Alain seemed to run a mental gambit, weighing decisions and their respective consequences against each other, carrying another weight and not breaking.

Roan continued, "Jovanis, Emery, Christian, myself. We were the first ones there. No one had yet made it to the rock. That makes it ours unless someone or something else follows it from the sky and claims it for themselves. It is ours and we need to ensure that. If it is gold and we do not claim it, we would be betraying ourselves and our people. We need to go put a guard around it until we can harvest it. We need to put a guard around it now. Unless someone else has gotten to it in the time we have been back here in the village. In case of that event, I am ready to fight for what is mine."

Alain spoke here and said, "Nothing is yours, Roan. Only a foolish man tries to hold the wind with a firm grip."

He paused for a minute, and Roan, headstrong and passionate, butted in and said, "It's not wind, it's—"

Alain held up an open palm to him indicating that he desired silence from Roan.

"All is wind," said Alain and then stood silent for a little more than a moment. "But," he continued, "we were first. We should accept and claim as much of this gift as we can, assuming it is what you say it is." By now, the sun they knew well had finished hiding itself behind the line on the horizon.

"We will not be able to get much done tonight. But we must keep an eye on this gift. You four. Your dedication to and many sacrifices for this tribe are documented with me and in the stars. Are you ready and willing to accept another task?"

They all, including Jovanis, nodded assuredly.

"We need you to watch this giant rock of gold this evening and until morning. At first light, every able-bodied man in the village will be at your side. We will assess and go from there. But remember, no man needs more than he needs. Once I know these good people here, under my watch, are satisfied and will be satisfied for the times to come, we will bless those around us just as we have been blessed, if this is what you say it is. Go. Prepare yourselves. Be pleased."

The four scouts quickly left for their respective homes and prepared to take on the new role of guard. They gathered some food rations and water for the evening, some bows and light spears. They felt excitement and trepidation. They somehow found a line between hustle and hesitation and walked it. The rest of the village had gone back to their own homes, more question than answer in their heads. Jovanis and his compatriots gathered at the northeast edge of the village and set forward toward their target.

PART IV

JOVANIS STOOD FIRM AS the hours of the night slipped silently by him. His back was almost warmed by the thought of the gilded meteorite at his back. Occasionally, he would reach back and place his hand firmly upon it. It was still there.

Early in the morning, Roan's voice rang out and called for a status update from all sides of the rock. One by one, the sentries reported that nothing was happening. Roan shouted in Rundi, "I cannot wait to dig into this thing!"

As the hours continued to creep and the golden gift sat silently behind him, Jovanis began to consider what it might mean to be rich. He entertained the idea that he would no longer need to wonder how he would pass the hours. The money would pass them without restriction or concern. His eyes gleamed like the gold silent behind him as steaks and fish and fancy drinks whirled around his head. Not only would his belly be full, but it would be full of the finest foods this world had to offer. And he would achieve these things without breaking a sweat. He could become content, finally, after so many years of perspiration. He thought of fancy shirts and pictured himself deciding whether to unbutton two or three of the top buttons to let his chest show. He thought of these things with certainty because the gold was at his back. It was secure. It was his.

No doubt worried his brow, and he bet on his riches in his mind as sure as the sun would rise.

Jovanis thought about white folk he had seen in town a few weeks before. It was safe to assume they were Christian missionaries despite their garb. They wore the costumes of his people. They did not wear the clothes of his people. They wore the costumes. With inauthenticity, they wore African clothing and handed out food, betrayed in their masquerade by the newness and the cleanliness of the clothes. But the white folk seemed happy. They could be whoever they wanted to be because they had the funds to do so. They could play dress-up and feel convinced in it. Their status afforded them no worries, and Jovanis wanted this. He wanted to be ignorant and happy. He wanted to play make-believe. He wanted to dress up like them for a day.

Jovanis thought on a magazine cover he had also seen in town. It had the image of a man who looked very nice. His hair was pristine, his clothes tailored. His eyes were shielded by sunglasses, and a drink sat in front of him. Bold, brash, yellow letters were stamped next to his face saying, "Horrible divorce!" but the man smiled. Jovanis wanted this too. If the man's wealth allowed him to smile through such problems, he wanted the problems. He wanted the wealth.

He thought about his mother and how she had never left Burundi. Neither of them had. They had both become content with it because they did not have the means to go anywhere else. Now, they might. He thought of leaving with his mother and seeing more of the world. He thought of big meals and nice shirts. He thought of a bed that he had seen in another magazine in town. He thought about buying one for himself and one for his mother.

Jovanis pictured himself lifted in silver and gold. He blissfully imagined and counted these things as veritable certainties because the rock was in his possession. It belonged to him and his people, and nothing could change that.

And suddenly, his reverie was interrupted by the whistling sound of a fast-moving projectile quickly approaching his location. With only seconds of warning, the whistle slammed into his chest and ejected all the air he held in his lungs. Jovanis gasped. Electricity erupted from the sudden, searing pain in his chest and followed along his veins throughout the course of his entire body. Fear and violence and heat and cold all congealed as he tried to gather what sudden horror might be happening to him. He looked down and saw a long wooden spear protruding from his torso. He gasped again, unable to hold any air in his lungs.

There were only questions in his mind as he reeled, and his eyes darted. "Who could have done this? Why is this happening? What do I do?"

He placed his hands around the spear, and with all the strength he could muster, he attempted to pull it from his bleeding chest. Electricity shot again through every nerve and muscle in him. The spear barely budged. He gasped again. No air comforted him. He heard shouts and battle cries start to fill the night sky around him.

Roan's mighty shout rang out in Rundi through the air, "We're under attack!"

Blackness like he had never known started to creep in from the edges of Jovanis' periphery. This was not like sleep. This was not like the night. This was far more permanent. He attempted one more gasp for air as he dropped to his knees, hands around the spear. No respite came. Jovanis saw his mother's face for a brief moment as the blackness continued to creep. Permanent night took him.

CHAPTER 19:

A STAGNANT POOL //

A ROARING RIVER //

CONFUSION SETS

THE NEXT FEW DAYS in Burundi saw civil war bud and bloom. Some of the less civilized tribes quickly turned to entitlement and war at the prospect of wealth. The ground around the golden rock became soaked with blood. And though blood was certainly shed, a good handful of people made it in and out of the area with a small chunk of gold and their lives. A man willing to take a very high risk could get rich in Burundi for those few days. Some said it was not worth it, but most of the people who said that had never been poor and had never lived in Africa.

Eventually, the United Nations sent troops into the area to attempt to gain control and get an understanding on the situation. A lot of the Burundians in the area refused to let the United Nations come in and block off access to the chunk of gold without a fight, and more lost their lives. Eventually the area was cleared and fenced off for research. The world needed to know where the rock came from, what it was, how it was, and why it was. Only then would it be decided what should be done with it and how it should be distributed. Thousands of Burundians surrounded the area, pressing their bodies up against the fence, kept from that which had fallen in their own backyard, from that which their friends and family members had recently lost their lives. Jovanis' mother stayed home in the village. The Ripple Six learned of the events from the news.

A weight fell over the group once they found out what happened. Peter was no longer looking up facts about humpback whales. Even Chester and Arch were solemn, smiling and cracking jokes far less than usual. What they had tried to do was so good in theory, but it had gone so horribly wrong, so horribly quickly.

As the news continued to boast the horrors taking place in Africa, seemingly wrought by their own hands, the Ripple Six had to wrestle with the devastating accuracy of Damien's words. No matter what they did nor what intention they may or may not have had, the countless crossing ley lines of fate and conflicting human volition would likely skew the intended trajectory of their actions. Things would rarely, if ever, proceed the way that they wished. They could do good, but what was to ultimately happen with their benevolence was up to the world. The best things, especially things of this magnitude, would often go awry in the hands of wicked and selfish men. This raised the question in their hearts: "Should we have done anything at all?"

Madeleine cried a few times a day, thinking of all the people that had now shuffled off this mortal coil because of them, because of her. Damien smoked much more than usual, but he did not cry. His mood did not seem to change much at all. When he found her crying, he would pull her close to him and say things like, "Baby, it's okay. It's all part of it," or "Death is a part of life." He would try to sweeten his words by taking her hair between his fingers and brushing it back behind her ears. None of it had the effect he intended in the throes of such sorrow. She knew these things to be true, but just because they were true did not mean she was not supposed to cry. These sorts of things were supposed to be cried over. She began to feel like she needed to lash out to get his attention, to get him to react to something, and she began pulling away from his hugs, responding with fewer and fewer words to the things he said, becoming more and more passive-aggressive. He was not shaking like she was. He was not hurting with her. Her pilot light would not ignite when she needed it to. She felt fully alone.

Damien continued to walk and speak and make decisions with confidence. He felt he needed to because Madeleine was reeling and relying on him. She had become so manic. He felt that he needed to stay calm. The stress solidified him and leaned him heavily into his belief system, which had let him survive psychologically this long, and he saw no need to adapt nor change. Madeleine was sure that change was exactly what she needed from Damien in that moment. He never asked her what she needed. She never told him. Things were getting confused and confusing.

As she lashed out, she failed to get his attention. He just continued to be her unwanted rock. She was hurting and he was hardening. She needed him to pull forward. He just sat and kept waving her into the intersection where she already sat vulnerable. He could not see that she needed him to move in that moment. He could not see that he needed to ignite. He could not see that he could just pull forward and push her out of the intersection or collide into her and end her spiraling. She would not tell him. She, in those moments, needed him to be more than human, whether he was constant or not, because her own humanity and the humanity of the world around her had failed.

Now, Peter was hurting just like Madeleine was. He was now directly responsible for death just like her. Unlike Damien, he had no answers. He had no understanding. He had no words. He did not even know the number of deaths for which he was responsible. He only had hurting. He hurt for the world, for humanity, for himself, and for Madeleine. Tears came to him often those few days as well.

As Damien went on unchanging, Madeleine went looking elsewhere for what she was not getting from him. In such uncertain times, uncertainty was all that she knew for certain. She could not understand how Damien could always be so sure that what he was saying was true. Everything but him seemed uncertain. She found more comforting uncertainty in Peter. She found empathy in him, and they began standing in the kitchen together more, talking about decisions and consequences, about the fragility of man, about how they would live with themselves. There was kinship in their responsibility for death and pain and in their lack of understanding. Peter did not try to make Madeleine stop hurting through philosophy. He did not try to convince her that there was beauty in pain. He just hurt with her. He reeled with her in the wake of their sudden ascension to godhood. On the second day, when they were standing in the kitchen, she put her hand on his for a moment as a tear fell from Peter's eye.

Later that second day, she happened upon an episode of the nature documentary series that featured river ecosystems. She began to think about different bodies of water.

A stagnant pool merits no divers, and a roaring river invites no swimmers. It's best to find a body in between. It is better to find a body of water with a solid input and a consistent output. She needed a stream in between. She needed a stream that changed subtly and consistently, but one that stayed the same in its core character. A stream thrives and does not kill nor die. It gives and lives and thrives and dies. It calmly flows. It simply is and ever was. Check the water. It's different than the day before, but not entirely. It's different than the day before, and still it flows.

Damien was at times the stagnant pool, at times the roaring river. He was not a gently flowing stream. He was a pilot light just sitting there. Metaphor upon metaphor stacked and swirled in her reeling mind. She could not tether her thoughts together like she should. They just moved and morphed into each other indecipherably. *Damien never mixes his metaphors,* she thought with unfounded certainty. Damien always mixed his metaphors.

Despite how he seemed, Damien was perpetually the roaring river in his thoughts. It just took a long time for anything to take hold. It took a long time for anything to breach the surface of the stagnant pool he carried on the outside. Occasionally, the most turbulent currents lay under the calmest surfaces. He never explained this to her. She never asked. Things were getting confused and confusing.

Peter, in those days, seemed to Madeleine to be a gently flowing stream.

On the third day after the event, they gathered at the apartment to be together and hopefully decide what they should do with the map. After an hour or so of talk, they came to no conclusions. They did not want to give it up and have it fall into someone else's hands quite yet. The new owner may face temptations unknown to the Ripple Six, far worse than they could ever imagine. It was hard to entertain the idea in light of what had happened, but the map in someone else's hands might be far more detrimental. Alternately, they could not destroy it because they were not quite sure what would happen if they did. They assumed nothing good. They were afraid to use it, even for "good," after the events in Burundi. The best-laid plans of mice and men and all that.

They decided to leave it be for the time being. They all needed to think both collectively and individually. It was not time to act. It was around dinnertime on the third day, and the group was starting to get hungry. Chester, Arch, Erin, and Damien decided to go get Chinese carry-out and bring it back to the apartment. Peter and Madeleine opted to stay back. They both found themselves a little too deep in thought, sorrow, and regret to leave. Damien asked Madeleine if she was sure she wanted to stay, and she insisted that she was.

As soon as the dinner-retrieval party closed the door, Madeleine looked at Peter. "Are we murderers?" she asked meekly.

"Yes and no," he said out the side of his mouth. A look of pity for her and for himself held in his brow. A small dimple sat in the center of his cheek. "I think murder implies intention. We did not want this to happen. You did not even know the map was capable of this. Sometimes you can't know the repercussions of your actions. We might be killers, but I don't think we're murderers."

"I don't want to feel this way." She grabbed his hand.

"I know," he said.

One tear began to well in his eye, and he let it flow calmly. She was comforted by his gentle outpour of emotion.

She leaned over and kissed him on the lips, feeling a comfort she had not felt since the map first came into their lives. He kissed back, counting, until he reached the number six and then pulled away.

She suddenly realized that the gently flowing stream was not so different from the pilot light. In fact, they were two versions of the same thing. They were both a power in between its full display. Power and strength at a certain point in time can seem like weakness or comfort, but the power is just keeping itself primed and ready for when it is needed. Then it springs to life and ignites or flows faster through the forest, depending on which metaphor is being used. Both the pilot light and the gently flowing stream were power seeming dormant at its particular point in time.

Then it occurred to her that these were people, not metaphors. In the nature of a true artist, in the nature of her beloved Damien, she had thought that she might be able to understand things further if she found herself able to connect things to other things. She had hoped the tethers of figurative language and thought would help her explain and get through her pain. But even after a handful of lovely metaphors, she still felt the pain and had in fact stacked more on top of it. She had some lovely word pictures to show, but a person was not a picture. A person is not static and complete like a picture. A person is ever changing. She was using another metaphor. She felt limited in her language. She felt like she was hopeless to ever understand. Things were getting confused and confusing.

Sweet Madeleine had never needed something different, nor had she found anything different at all. She had simply needed Damien to utilize his power differently. She had gone off searching for something she already had when she could have just talked to him. She could have just asked him to ignite. She filled with regret. She had made another huge mistake. Things were getting confused and confusing.

CHAPTER 20:

I WILL BE THERE FOR YOU

THE NEXT DAY, MADELEINE lay on the couch watching *Friends* for hours. The boys were at work, and she had the day off. She had photos she could be editing, but instead, she lay on the couch watching *Friends*, episode after episode.

When she kissed Peter, he kissed back for six seconds before he pulled away. "We should not be doing this," he whispered to her. She did not say anything. The stillness held thick around them, restraining time as well as space. "We can't," he whispered again, this time with resolve, saying it as much to himself as to her. Then he stood and flew like a bat out of hell from the room.

When she kissed Peter, she had been kissing a need of hers, not the man, Peter, himself. She was kissing an escape from pain. She was kissing pain itself, trying to show it love because hating it did not seem to be working. She was kissing an idea. She was kissing something that seemed different. When she kissed Damien the last few days, it felt the same as it always had. It felt constant and boring, but maybe she needed constant and boring. As tempestuous as the last few days had been, perhaps she should have stayed at the port she knew, not floated aimlessly at sea, looking for new places to dock.

An episode of *Friends* ended in front of her, and it must have been the third because Netflix asked if she was still watching. She chose yes.

Damien had always been there, though he had not always been exactly what she needed him to be when he was there. She could not decide which was better: there and imperfect or perfect and not there. Then she realized that if it was not there, she could not know if it was perfect or imperfect, what she wanted or not. She could only be sure about the thing that was there. Damien was always there. He was her rock. He stood throughout time, unwavering and trustworthy, constant in his resolve.

At that moment, Damien thought about whether he should text Madeleine. He did not want to bug or overwhelm her, but she needed his help. But maybe he could help better by giving her some space. But she seemed to like when he was there for her. He decided to text her. He typed, "I love you baby. I know you're hurting. Let it grow you. Embrace it. It will make you stronger." Then he deleted it. Then he typed it again. Then he sent it. The whole process of contemplation, decision, and execution took about five minutes.

Madeleine received the text and sunk a bit deeper into the couch. He was there, but maybe she did not need him to be. Maybe she needed someone to let her break. Maybe she did not need to be made stronger, not at a moment like this. But he was there. She looked at the message again and felt comfort. He was there for her.

Madeleine turned her attention back to *Friends*. She watched a few episodes without hazarding any original thoughts of her own and realized something. Each of the episodes was centered on one of the characters hiding something and deceiving the other Friends. There was an episode about Rachel trying to convince Phoebe that an apothecary table she purchased from Pottery Barn came from a flea market. There was one where Joey tried to hide that a movie in which he had been cast had been cancelled. There was an entire season where Chandler and Monica tried to hide that they were dating. There was season after season of laughter at the expense of their souls as they lied and deceived and hid from each other, and she wanted no part of it.

She felt the hold these lies had in her heart. For a good majority of her young life, she had been formed by television. It was her unintended Bible. She never sat down in front of it with the purpose of gleaning truth or shaping her soul, but she spent more time in front of it than any other source of information. To think it was not shaping her would be ludicrous. It would be ignorant. It would be like eating a daily loaf of bread and then looking at the accumulating pounds with indignation.

In television, she had been enamored by conflict. She was captivated by the conflict the television fed her, and she blissfully consumed all that it could distribute. It was conflict stemmed in dishonesty. Deceitful conflict called to her, and she came running and stayed in conflict's house for hours at a time. Conflict seemed to attract attention. She did not want to attract attention. She wanted to watch others as they were, naturally, without a show, and she could not do that if they were abundantly aware of her presence, which they would be if she was draped in dishonesty. So she did not want to stay in conflict. She did not want to live in dishonesty. The lives and stories to which she had dedicated her own life for so long suddenly repulsed her. She had been consuming poison. She turned the television off.

She decided that she had to tell Damien what she had done. She prayed to God (something she had not done in a long time) that it would not break him. She had to tell him. If he wanted to be there for her, he had to be there in this too, in her failing. In fact, if he truly believed that pain was gain, he would look at this incident favorably. Wouldn't he? She prayed again. This would either solidify his belief system and their relationship or break him, and either of those outcomes would be beneficial. If he broke, it would prove that his worldview was false and unsustainable, and either way, everyone would come out on top. Either way, she had to tell him. He was her best friend – and not a friend like on the television. She no longer wanted truth from the television. She wanted truth from Damien. She and Damien loved and trusted each other, or at least they used to. They gave to each other as much as they got from each other, or at least they used to. When one was weak, the other was strong. She just prayed he was strong unless he did not need to be. She was beginning to sound like Damien.

CHAPTER 21:

DATING A MURDERER

MADELEINE LAY IN BED with Damien that evening and traced the shadows she saw on the wall onto his chest. A light beyond the tree outside his window projected intricate shadows into the room. Touching him felt like a betrayal. She was no longer his exclusively. With the infidelity between them, it felt as if she was not actually touching him at all. It was as if there was a film keeping her finger from his chest.

"I don't want to hurt anymore."

"Then don't hurt," he responded matter-of-factly and closed the leather notebook in which he was scrawling. "It only hurts if you let it. Think of hurt as healing. Think of pain as gain. Then hurt does not hurt. Think of—"

"Stop. You didn't kill anyone, Damien. It baffles me that you always think you know what you're talking about."

If only she knew his thought life.

"I don't. I'm sorry. If only you knew my thought life. I am always doubting myself. Every moment, I argue with myself. The fact I say anything at all is a miracle. I'm so sorry. I ... Anything I say is just what I feel is right. I just wanted to help. I don't want you to hurt. I imagine that you have to."

She looked him clean in the eyes. She hardly believed his words. Just like that, Damien had finally reached where she needed him. He realized that she had to hurt. But as Arch would say, "You can't unring a bell." The following words still had to happen. She still had to tell him. The tears rushed to her eyes.

"Baby?"

"I kissed Peter."

The shadow on the wall seemed to flex like a ghastly hand. He quickly looked down. His head twitched to the left a bit. Then his head twitched to the right two times. Then he frowned. Then he blinked six times. His lips were parted slightly, and he carried the weight of all of it in his brow. The shadows on the wall shifted. The film between her and him dissipated, and it burned.

He had prepared himself for this moment. His whole life and ideology had prepared him for pain like this. He knew that pain was gain, that it would grow him. He had now seen the other side of the coin and it was good, but it hurt. It really hurt. No book, no podcast, no number of songs written could prepare him fully for this actual feeling. His chest tightened and seemed to almost implode into itself. A black hole opened where his heart once was and began creating a void. There was no accounting for pain like this. There was neither explanation nor rationalization that he could find in the corners of his mind. It was as if he read about water his entire life and then drowned the first time he went for a swim.

"Why?"

"I don't know, Damien." The tears had moved far past welling. They began to pour. Her lip quivered. "I don't know and I'm so sorry. I couldn't hear anymore that it was okay. That I was supposed to hurt. That it was supposed to happen. Was I supposed to wipe out a city?"

Damien resisted an urge to correct her. Colmar was actually a town.

"I can imagine that bad things are beneficial, Damien. I really can. I understand that it grows you and shapes you into something stronger.

Forged by fire, right? But I needed you to stop telling me it was fine. Just because it's good doesn't mean it's …" she trailed, "… not bad. I didn't need a philosophy lesson. I needed some empathy.

"Sometimes the glass isn't half-full or half-empty," she continued. "Sometimes it doesn't matter at all how it's perceived. Sometimes there truly is more than half the cup filled, and sometimes there truly is less than half the cup filled. It's important to see the cup as it truly is, which takes time and discernment. And sometimes there's no cup at all. And sometimes, no water. This is beyond understanding or explanation. This really hurts. You cannot just have a preprogrammed response for everything, Damien."

People tend to talk too much or too little in the face of a tragedy. Pain this poignant is unnatural and makes people fumble with proper response protocol. But that did not mean that what she was saying was wrong. In fact, it struck Damien with unprecedented profundity.

"Peter's the only one that understood what I was going through. What I *am* going through. Or so I thought." The tears flowed like a raging river. She rambled a bit a bit more and tried to touch his face. He pulled away a bit and stared at the shadows on the wall. "You are my rock, Damien. My rock. For a minute, in the moment, you were too constant. I needed you to cry with me. I needed you to hurt for me and with me. I thought I needed him but I didn't. I needed you. I just needed you not to be so sure. I needed you to ignite and hate with me. You're dating a murderer, Damien. A mass murderer. I hate this map. I hate it. I needed you to cry with me."

"Well, I'm crying with you now," he said without tears in his eyes.

"I am so sorry."

There was silence. It was bigger than a kiss. He was hurting, and he could not find the good in it. His very essence was starting to shake and crumble. Damien pulled away and crawled to the end of the bed where he sat cross-legged.

"Can you forgive me?" said Madeleine. It was minor if he even moved at all, but Madeleine would swear she saw Damien shake his head no.

They sat with each other for another hour. They talked sparingly about how things could have happened differently. They both found things they should have done or not done. A good portion of the hour was spent in silence. Damien pointed out a few times that looking back did not change the fact that something had happened.

"This is over," Damien finally said. He had decided the moment she told him.

"Damien, no." She wept.

"I can't trust you anymore, Madeleine. I'm sorry. I am. But kissing you now would kill me. I'm sorry I wasn't enough for you."

She wept harder. "I'm so sorry. I'm so sorry."

Damien let her cry for a while then asked her to leave. He assured her that he had loved her and mercilessly put an emphasis on the past tense. He wanted to see her writhe. She wept harder – to the point that she thought she might run dry – but the tears kept coming.

The events of that evening raced by at faster and faster speeds. Neither of them wanted to hold on to anything that was happening or cherish a single moment of it; they only wanted to get through. So no moment stuck with them, and time seemed to pass by like a train: loud, disorienting, and fast.

Damien led Madeleine to the front door and into the night. He wanted her to feel rejected. He wanted her to hurt like he was hurting. He closed the door and heard her cry fade into the night. She went home.

Damien laid his head on his pillow. There were a few wet spots from Madeleine's tears. He turned the pillow over. He looked at the wall, and the shadows shifted. *Everything has to change eventually,* he thought to himself. He knew change well. His mind changed endlessly from day to day. But now it was not shifting like it did before. Things were beginning to congeal. It was over.

Despite his usual proclivity for entertaining new thoughts to survive, he found it impossible to change his stance toward Madeleine. It was over the moment she told him what she had done. For maybe the first time in his life, he felt the decision truly solidify in the vacuum where his heart once was. The pain hardened like happy concrete around the decision to end things with sweet Madeleine, and the shadows no longer shifted on the wall. He did not move.

CHAPTER 22:

TYRANTS OF TALK

DAMIEN AWOKE IN AN audience. Such drastic sights and sounds greeted him there that he was immediately thrown into a panic. All around him was a swirling, pulsating, convulsing sea of bodies, thousands of human beings swaying forward and back like seagrass. The bodies heaved and pulled, back and forth unceasingly. He tried to catch his breath. He noticed that he was seated and looked down. Under him was a burgundy, cushioned theatre seat. He looked around. Under each body was an identical burgundy, cushioned theatre seat. Despite the disorienting barrage of sights and sounds, he continued to scan the crowd and gather his bearings. The people were all different. There were men, women, and children of all colors, shapes, and sizes, but they all shared one horrible feature in common. Upon each face was a hideous, twisted grin. The corners of each mouth seemed to flee from the center of each head, appearing to almost rip each face in twain in a demonic, clownish grin. Back and forth they swayed. The horrible bodies pulsed and swayed and smiled and shook all around him.

Then there was the sound, a wall of cacophonous sound that caused his head to throb, making it hard to immediately identify what was happening. His ears felt hot, and his vision blurred. After a few moments, after witnessing the people writhing back and forth and grinning maniacally, he finally put his finger on the noise. Each hideous, grinning face released an equally hideous, deafening laugh. Screams, shouts, and cackles of bliss tore through the room in all directions. Where the audience should have been running out of breath or stopping their roaring guffaws, they seemed only to get louder. Damien was shaken to his very core.

He looked around desperately, hoping to find why or how he had gotten there. No immediate answer came, but he was able to notice more about his surroundings. The theatre had three tiers, and he was on the third. Below him were two more sections of the horrible, chortling seagrass people. They were all different in their dress, color, shape, and size. They were all the same in their perverted merriment. The theatre was plain. Burgundy panes of soundproofing material ran along the walls, and there were small theatre lights but not much more in the way of decoration. He looked up, expecting to see catwalks, bridges, and lights, but there were none to be found. The theatre seemingly had no ceiling, and he peered into eerie blackness.

As he focused his gaze back down past the sea of people, he finally brought his eyes to the stage. Upon it were five men at a table covered in a black cloth. They sat at the table looking back and forth, gesticulating and moving their mouths as if a conversation were happening, but no sound rose above the hideous laughter. Occasionally they seemed to laugh themselves, but then they would stop and continue moving their mouths in the manner of speaking. None of them seemed to be listening. They all talked unceasingly and moved their hands around.

The crowd began noticeably reaching for the stage.

Damien cried out, "Stop! Stop laughing! What are you all doing!? What is so funny!?" The laughter only grew louder. His words were drowned as soon as they left his mouth. He looked at the person to his left, a small, middle-aged Asian woman with a bob, and he tried to grab her. As he reached for her arms to grab her and shake her from her laughter, she pulled away from him. She and the space she occupied all seemed to slide away from him, the matter between him and her pulling and stretching like taffy as his arms grasped at air. She continued laughing and heaving toward the stage. He turned to the man on his right, a young man about his age, very athletic with a clean haircut and beard. He reached for this man as well, and space itself seemed to stretch again, pulling the man and the crowd around him from Damien's grasp. But as Damien's arms returned to his sides, the man seemed to be exactly where he had been before, sitting directly next to the now terrified Damien.

He looked back at the stage, and all five men were continuing to move their mouths and talk all at the same time.

By now the people were not only reaching for the stage; they were beginning to leave their seats. Arms swinging wildly forward, some of the audience began to stand and crawl over the people and seats in front of them. He looked past the man to his right and saw a young woman in the front row of the third-tier balcony in which he was seated. She stood up, reached forward, and threw herself off the balcony. Then another man past her crawled over the four rows of people between him and the stage and dove off the balcony with arms outstretched. Damien, panicked and afraid, looked to his left and saw the Asian woman he had tried to shake free. Laughing, she threw herself into the crowd below. One by one, the crowd began crawling and surging forward in pursuit of the five men onstage, hurling themselves over the other members of the crowd and off the balconies in front of them.

"Stop!" he screamed again and again. He continued to scream at the mass of laughing fans to no avail as they surged forward. The first wave of people finally reached the men onstage and did not stop. They crawled on top of the table and then on top of the men themselves. The audience piled one by one on top of the men onstage. Writhing and laughing, the pile grew and grew in the middle of the stage. Damien screamed and screamed. Laughter filled his ears and mind to the point that he thought he might burst, and then, suddenly, he woke up screaming, alone in his room.

CHAPTER 23:

IF YOU NEED TO ASK

"THIS ISN'T RIGHT. WE should be together. You always talk of how people fail, and then you bail as soon as I do. I don't understand how this is any different. I'm sorry. Please forgive me, Damien. Until you do, I can't be in Indiana. I'm going to stay with friends in Portland until I hear from you. Please. Forgive me. Don't touch the map."

Damien read Madeleine's text message repeatedly over the course of the next couple days, but he did not text her back. He moped around the apartment, dragging his feet everywhere he went. Without her, he no longer had his lift. He had nothing pulling him up. He drank and smoked more than ever before and hardly spoke to Chester and Arch. They did not push him. He was full of hate. He hated her. He hated Peter. He hated himself, so he punished himself with poison and pouting.

The map seemed to taunt him from the wall. It was not Peter that stole his girlfriend. It was that map. It had broken her and stolen her loyalty. Every time he passed it to return to the kitchen for another beer, it jeered at him from its place on the wall. He wished he had never found it.

Damien hurt. He hurt fiercely. For all his philosophical tussling and rational thought, he had believed he understood everything. He knew how to think. He knew how to approach everything he encountered philosophically except this pain. In theory, he should be able to explain away the pain. If he understood it, he had power over it. All he needed was its name to gain control of the beast. And he tried. But it hurt him. Try as he might, he could not explain away the pain. It still burned like a hot coal in his chest. He could not understand why he hurt the way he did, and that fact hurt him even more.

One evening, he was lying facedown on the floor in his room surrounded by beer bottles when a knock rang out from his bedroom door.

"Come in."

It was Arch. He held a half gallon of whiskey in his left hand. The smell of pizza came calling from the main room. "Come on, man. We're done with this. No more pouting. She sucks. Come play video games with Chester and I."

Damien lay there for a second and then got up without saying a word. A slight groan emanated from his chest. He followed Arch into the family room where the map sneered at him from the wall.

"I got your girl," the map said to him.

"I'm going outside to smoke," said Damien. The map made his skin crawl. He could not be in that room.

"Just sit down and smoke inside tonight," said Chester through a mouthful of pizza.

Damien lit a cigarette and removed the cap from the half gallon of whiskey. He threw it back. The whiskey seduced him, caressed him, undressed him. For a moment, he felt warm and safe, but those feelings faded as fast as they came. The pain returned and draped over him again like a cloak. He threw back another swallow.

The night rolled by at an exponentially increasing pace as their indulgence caused time to snowball. It was getting late. They smoked and drank and ate pizza and badmouthed Madeleine and Peter. The bottle was beginning to be bested. Damien felt himself start to bend as the whiskey removed him from himself.

He hated her. She was the only good thing he had, and she left him. She betrayed him for that goody good, Peter. His veins bulged as emotion filled him and had nowhere to go. He tried not to shake so the guys would not see, but he was filling to the brim. He lit another cigarette and threw back more whiskey. She was always going to do this. It was no surprise. She was broken as they all were, and the betrayal should have come as sure as sunrise. But it hurt. Oh, it hurt. His chest felt tight, and he gritted his teeth. He ripped smoke from his cigarette as hard as he could and winced. All he knew now was pain. How could he be this drunk and still hurt this much? How was he feeling anything at all? It was always going to happen. She did it to him. He did it to him. It did it to him. He thought he knew her. His thoughts started to melt together and blur and make less sense. It hurt. Oh, it hurt. This was always going to happen. He could handle it because pain was always in the cards.

He started rocking back and forth on the couch. Chester and Arch were staring at their hurting friend.

Damien grabbed a slice of pizza and hurled it at the ceiling. He stood up, threw his head back, and screamed into the heavens. "You cannot shock me! You cannot hurt me!" Chester and Arch reeled back, shocked by the outburst. "There's nothing new under the sun, right? Right! She was always going to do this to me! We were always going to fail! Good. Good!" He teetered back and forth from the drink, boasting immunity to pain for the recurrent nature of human events.

He whirled around and looked at the map with malice like he had never felt before. He hated viciously in that moment. Life, God, little green men – whatever it was – something had brought him to this place of hurt, and he no longer desired to live there. He looked at the map and realized what he could do. He could end it all. Hurt, decisions, stupidity ... he could take it all away in one fell swoop. But he squashed the thought promptly. What a horrible thought it was.

But with Damien's drunken outburst at the heavens followed by sudden, stoned silence, Arch felt it was time for him to spring to action. His friend needed him to fight. He stood up and muttered, "That's it. She's not hurting you anymore." He grabbed the cigarette from the corner of Damien's mouth and drove it directly into the dot marked Portland.

All of a sudden, everyone in Portland felt very hot. Then they felt nothing at all.

Damien screamed at the top of his lungs. There was a pulse from the map that knocked Arch backwards over the coffee table. Chester tried to catch him but was not quick enough. There was chaos in the room, and Damien blinked his eyes and looked at the map. Sure enough, a black, smoldering hole now sat where Portland once did. Damien jumped over the table directly onto Arch's chest, and they both rolled onto the floor.

He screamed, "What have you done?" into Arch's face and threw his fists forward, hitting Arch repeatedly in the face and chest. After a few seconds, he redirected one of his fists to the floor next to Arch's head, stamping the carpet with blood from Arch's nose.

"What have you done? What have you done? You aren't God, Arch. You can't just do that." He grabbed Arch by the shoulders and shook him. Chester grabbed Damien by the shoulders and tried to pull him off his friend. Damien shook free with ease and pushed Chester back, empowered by his rage and blood alcohol concentration.

"I was just trying to help, Damien! We're the ones with the map after all! What's the difference between us and God!?" Arch screamed as he tried to put his hands in front of his face.

Damien stopped. Everyone stopped. They all breathed for a moment. Blood boiled behind Damien's eyes, and his shoulders rose and fell. He set his jaw and looked Arch dead in the eyes. It felt as if Damien was looking directly through him. Damien opened his mouth and spoke.

"God wouldn't need to ask that question."

The three young men got up off the floor and began straightening things a bit. Damien took the map carefully off the wall and put it behind the couch. The world around them seemed to shiver.

"Maybe it didn't work," said Chester.

There was a bit of silence.

"I really hope not," said Damien.

Arch did not say anything at all. The three young men could not believe what had just happened. It was too quick. How could that have happened that quickly? Something so horrible should take much longer. It was surreal. Never before had they wished so severely that what was happening was not happening.

Arch pulled out his phone and googled Portland. Headline after headline confirmed that he had succeeded in his act of divine retribution. Portland and its surrounding areas had burst into flames just minutes before. A perfect circle of scorched earth lay where the bustling metropolis of weird and wander once thrived.

"What have I done?" he whispered and handed his phone to Damien.

Damien did not say a word. He considered calling the police on Arch. He looked at him again. He could not deal with it tonight. His whiskey jacket would not let the reality of this information in.

"I'm going to sleep," he said drunkenly. "We'll deal with this in the morning."

The three all stumbled to their own respective rooms and laid their heads on their own respective beds. Chester and Arch drenched their own respective pillows with tears. Damien tried to come to terms with the fact that Madeleine was gone. He would never see her again. And she had died unforgiven by him.

He began to think about instruments of destruction right before the slumber took him. He could not help but think about gun control. He thought about the "guns do not kill people, people kill people" argument and found it imbecilic. Guns do not kill people, and people do not kill people. People with guns kill people. People are going to kill people one way or another. The easier murder is made through the possession of powerful tools, the more the temptation will grow, and the more murder will occur. When elevated by things, people and places in the material realm have all their attributes amplified. It was not the map that killed people, and it was not Arch that killed people. It was the map in Arch's trembling hands that killed people. Great power in foolish hands becomes foolish.

CHAPTER 24:

NUMEROLOGY

PETER SAT ON HIS bed with his guitar in his hands. It had six strings. He plucked them one by one from the bottom to the top and counted to six. He did it again. He kept doing it until he had done it sixty-six times. A portal to hell did not open.

Peter-Peter-girlfriend-stealer was reeling. How could he be so wicked? What he had done to Damien, to Madeleine, to the good Lord, to himself – it felt unforgivable. He had been told that there was forgiveness for everything, but this felt beyond. This was a betrayal of the highest order. Peter thought of the ninth circle of Hell in Dante's "Inferno." There, in the center, were the betrayers: Satan himself chewing on Brutus, Judas, and Cassius. Peter belonged in one of Satan's mouths with the rest of them. He should be frozen and chewed on by the beast forever.

Peter thought about the number nine. It was relatively unsymbolic as far as he could remember, whereas every other single digit number had a myriad of different meanings. Two may be the other most unsymbolic single digit number, but he was not thinking about two right now. He was thinking about nine.

There were nine realms of contrapasso in the "Inferno." Ferris Bueller had missed school nine times when Ed Rooney called Ferris's mom. There were nine rings, nine wraiths, and nine companions of the Fellowship of the Ring in J.R.R. Tolkien's *Lord of the Rings* book series. When people were elated, they were said to be on cloud nine. There were nine types of angels in the Bible. He had nine posters hanging in his room. He thought through all the times he had noticed the number nine in his life and tried to tether them together. He could not find anything particularly consistent.

The number one represented unity. It was the ultimate number. It was first in lists and above all else, though somehow also below.

Two was a little harder to pin down. Two was the number of each species of animal ushered onto the ark. It was also the number of tablets on which the Ten Commandments were written. Each person had two hands, two nostrils, two eyes, two ears, but they had only one brain. It was said that two brains are better than one. Perhaps that was why people got into romantic relationships: they needed another brain. Two was the typical number of people that would join into a romantic relationship.

Three was maybe most significant of all single digit numbers. God was three persons in one. Things complemented each other in groups of threes and then found themselves complete. Sky, earth, and water formed the seemingly complete world around him. Time was broken into the past, present, and future. Each person was made up of body, mind, and soul.

Four seasons, four elements, four corners of the earth. Peter's mind was trying to quantify reality and was beginning to buckle a little. These numbers had to mean something. He needed something to latch onto. Maybe if he had kissed Madeleine for seven seconds instead of six, it would have been holy. Was it the number that made something sacred or something sacred that brought value to the number? He counted to six with his lips upon hers. If he had pushed through for one more second, would he have felt that need to flee? Could he have held for one more second even if he wanted to? Was the number decided for him?

The number five now came to his mind. The great Pythagoras was known to have said, "All is number" and that the number five was the perfect number of the human microcosm. Practicing Hindus believed that there were five elements instead of four, and the goddess of knowledge, Saraswati, was associated with the number five. In Discordianism, the Law of Fives stated that all things happened in fives. The five-pointed pentagram bore significance in many religions, especially Satanism. Peter got a little spooked just thinking of the Prince of Darkness. Five must not be good.

Six came to his mind, and he skipped it. He had no more mental capacity for six.

Seven met his synapses like a new down comforter. He felt so safe in its folds. Lucky number seven had been full of so much providence in the lives of his gambling friends. God had created this sweet world in seven days. "Seven, seven, seven" flashed so clearly across his mind it could be seen in his eyes like a cartoon character playing the slots. There were seven notes in the diatonic scale. He had learned that from Damien. The number of times that he could recall seven in the Bible was far more than seven. But then it darkened. There were seven deadly sins. There were seven things that were detestable to the Lord. Seven demons were driven out of Mary Magdalene. He saw seven in a new light or, to be more accurate, a new lack of light. Perhaps seven was not so holy. Perhaps it was not so good. The world was created in seven days.

He had to move to eight. Six and seven were killing him.

"Why was six afraid of seven?" he asked himself. "Because seven eight nine."

He considered for a moment that he should just laugh at these numbers and that they all meant nothing at all. But then there was eight.

The number eight was perfect. Turned on its side, it told the time of forever. He had read that in ancient Egypt it was the number of balance and cosmic order. Perhaps balance came in death and rebirth. In Biblical numerology, the number eight signified resurrection and regeneration. It came right after seven, the number of days God took to completely create everything. Eight came after everything. So eight signified a new beginning. The eighth note was where the diatonic scale started over. Peter was coming back. He had died in six and seven, and now he was being brought back to life just in time for number nine.

Peter thought over the number nine. So often he had seen it in film and literature. Maybe this number was from and for man. Maybe it was defined in the fact that it could forever be defined. Man used the number nine to tell the story of being man, of needing a number. There were nine personality types in the Enneagram of personality. All of man can be summed up in nine. He started to feel so good about nine. He started to take solace in nine. But then again, there were nine circles in hell. But then again, nine summed up man, and he had kissed his best friend's girlfriend.

Peter looked around his room and counted nine blue DVDs in his DVD collection. He saw nine records lying on the floor next to his record shelf. He once again counted the nine posters on the wall. Nine jumped from the walls around him, and he did nothing more than ask, "What could it mean?"

He hurt. He looked. He came back to confusion. These numbers seemed to contradict themselves just as he daily did. Maybe the numbers were a reflection of him. Maybe he was a reflection of the numbers. Maybe some things mean nothing at all.

Eight snowflakes fell outside his window.

CHAPTER 25:

COR DEI, PART 2

THAT NIGHT, DAMIEN HAD the last dream he would ever have.

He awoke once again within a clutter of color and lines. Looking around, he recognized the celestial stew he had swum through just days before. He saw the swirling, swimming lines of every conceivable hue within the entire color spectrum and some for which he had no name. He remembered immediately and relived the vast flux of emotion he felt in every breaking moment. Once again, this was home and this was God.

Damien remembered his previous adventure and his lesson in freedom. He promised the lines he would not try to structure them this time. He was there to appreciate. He was there to take part in the holy celebration of complexity and limitlessness.

He took a deep breath, and even the air he inhaled felt colorful. His lungs tingled with delight as he drank of the space around him, and he was ready to explore. With an excited shout, he threw himself through the godheart. He knew how to navigate it this time. He did barrel rolls and somersaults. He swung from line to line, finding colors he had never seen before. He laughed. He cried. He shouted with delight as he lived and learned.

His excitement grew. He could hardly contain himself. How was it that he – the broken, destitute, stupid, moody man that he was – could be allowed to take part in such a symphony of color and freedom? "Thank you!" he shouted. He got to take part! He wanted to take in every aspect of it and began to grab the strings even tighter as he swung past. He could not miss a single feeling. Then he grabbed one string even tighter. Then he grabbed another even tighter. The strings almost began to groan as he grabbed them with such horrible fervor. He frowned and looked around. He could have sworn he heard a groan. But then he saw the lines again and was brought back to bliss. What beauty! What color! What freedom! He continued to swing and flip and barrel roll his way through the chromatic jungle, feeling more and more freedom with each passing moment.

As Damien swung by a particularly delicious-looking shade of blue, he found that he could no longer contain himself. He had always liked blue-colored foods. He took a bite from the string, and he bit clean through. There was an audible snap and then a groan, but it was incomparably delicious. What flavor! He had never known a flavor so vibrant. He continued swinging and biting and pulling his way through strings. He ripped a few in half and began laughing, and as he did, the lines began to slacken. Around him, the strings all began to fall and thicken around him. As they fell through the space, the space lessened. He was beginning to be crushed under the weight of the strings, now so close together that he could hardly discern one color from the next. They all seemed to congeal into one painfully dull shade of brown.

He realized he had once again gone too far. He had taken far too many liberties with the space. The weight of the fallen lines was crushing him flat. His bones began to groan beneath the insufferable mass of his mistake.

"I am so sorry," he said quietly to the mass around him. "I went too far. I see that now."

A breath seemed to come into the mass. With a gasp, the color seemed to flicker and fill the mass. It began to separate. There, a line. There, a color. It was not too late.

As the lines were revivified, Damien felt hope. Twice now he had ruined the space, but twice now the space had still survived. Once he had destroyed it with structure, and once he had destroyed it with freedom. He had to find a way to interact with it between absolute freedom and absolute structure. He needed to find an approach, it seemed, far less absolute. It was tough. The space was so beautiful, vibrant, and alive. He could not react but extremely. Every reaction he had to it seemed to be wrong. His reactions were too much. But how was he supposed to react? Perhaps this would forever be the nature of their relationship. He would fail time and time again, but the space would survive. The space was enough to endure his folly. It was beautiful for that.

"I am sorry," he said again. There seemed to be another inhalation in the room.

The lines continued to separate and become themselves again. Vibrant color filled them once more. In light of his two-parted blunder in the space, he now sat amongst the lines quietly. Moments passed and turned into seconds. The seconds turned into minutes. The minutes turned into hours. He finally let himself be still amidst the celestial symphony of color and line. He closed his eyes and felt the warm threads again brush his skin, thrilling him and burning his heart to a happy cinder. He felt his very self washed away, to be replaced again with another version of his self.

This time he was slightly different. This time he felt no need to react. He had no desire to stamp or mark the space in any way, and the lines continued to swirl around him. It was enough without him, but still he was allowed to swim amongst the beauty. Tears streamed down his cheeks. The dancing lines seemed to change their flow a bit and began to incorporate him in their movement. They led his limbs in their swirl. He joined the godheart in a dance unlike any he had seen or taken part in before. It felt directionless and choreographed all at once. It was at one time chaotic and meticulously purposed. It was a beautiful contradiction, and he danced and cried and felt more alive than he ever had before.

He danced all night until he woke up to faint traces of sunlight creeping in the window. His bliss was promptly replaced with pain from a hangover.

CHAPTER 26:

DAMIEN: DARK ORIGINS

IT WAS NOT A matter of forgiveness. He forgave her. He forgave her and would have forgiven her time and time again if he was given the chance. He had seen the tides of human morality and capability flow in and out too many times to be surprised that she had made a mistake. It was a matter of whether he could trust her in the future. He could not. In fact, he should have never trusted her at all. He should never trust anyone.

Damien lay in bed early the following morning. He had not looked at the clock yet, but the sun was just starting to softly smile through the window. Damien thought it was extremely inappropriate for the sun to be shining. He could not have slept for more than a couple hours.

It was his fault for putting her on a pedestal in the first place. No man or woman that has ever walked this sullied globe deserved an esteemed position. They all fell. They all served only themselves. They all deserved to fall. They all fell before they ever stood up.

> I'll build your silly cities
> I'll build and watch them fall
> In fact, they've always fallen
> They never stood at all

I'll build your silly cities
Of Legos, cups and dirt
I'll watch them all fall one by one
Condemned by their own birth

It's all dirt it's all dirt it's all dirt it's all dirt
It's all dirt it's all dirt it's all dirt it's all dirt
It's all dirt it's all dirt it's all dirt it's all dirt
It's all dirt it's all dirt it's all dirt

If everyone was fallen, unworthy of esteem, that included him. Madeleine had elevated him because of his love, his music, his writing, his alternative worldview, and he had fallen in her sight because he was never meant to have been raised so high. He was elevated by another thing. He was elevated by the map. He was elevated by the power it possessed. The power was his, and he had not the capacity to use it wisely because there was no wisdom in him.

Damien's mind then took a leap – a leap he had taken before and quickly negated. This time, in wake of the night before, he let the thought take hold. Damien decided on destruction.

This instrument of his and all of humanity's ineptitude could no longer stand. The map needed to be destroyed. It needed to be ensured that never again could humanity's fallen nature and certain failure be amplified so far and so wide.

The villain chapter was being written in Damien's heart. This was his twilight turning. This was the full moon of his heart emerging from behind a clouded veil. This moment would someday be retold at the end of a graphic novel titled *Damien: Dark Origins*.

Now, how would he do this? This new Damien – quick to make decisions, free from endless waffling – was far more efficient than the one before. This Damien got things done. He would love to use an element. They seemed the most poetic and powerful of destroyers. He scrolled through the elements in his head.

He could not destroy it with wind. As far as he knew, something had to enter the map to have any effect. He thought back to his friend, Peter, speaking into the map. It somehow felt like months had passed. Peter-Peter-girlfriend-stealer. He forgave Peter, but Peter was fallen, human, and needed to go just like the rest of them. Peter deserved to die. He would need something a bit more corporeal than wind. Before moving on, he entertained for a moment the idea of all of humanity being blown off the face of the earth and into outer space, and it made him happy. And there they shall float in their iniquity, without direction or hope, forevermore.

He considered using water. A cleansing flood would be just as effective as it was metaphorical. But he recalled a Bible verse in which God promised never to flood the earth again, and since he was God now, he would keep His promise.

He pictured lighting the four corners of the world with his lighter and letting it burn itself in from its edges. He saw the fire crawling slowly across the face of the earth and the people running from the walls of flame. He saw the last, unconsumed people of earth gathering at the very center, hugging and screaming as the blazing tidal waves inched ever closer. But he was afraid that a simple breeze would put the fire out after he had been consumed and leave some of the world and people of it standing undestroyed.

His obliteration-centric process of elimination eventually left him with only one option: earth. The word met his mind, and it made perfect sense. From dirt we were born, and to dirt we would return. He could cover the entire planet in dirt in one fell swoop and crush every single breathing, pitiful, sickening human being. Plus, there would still be non-human life in the soil that could potentially become something good in the future. There was hope in this decision.

CHAPTER 27:

THE OUTFIT IN WHICH

HE WOULD BE BURIED

DAMIEN GATHERED HIMSELF OVER the course of the next few minutes. He slid his legs into the same pair of tattered, old blue jeans he had been wearing for the last week and patted the pocket to make sure his cigarettes were still there. They were. He pulled open the drawer that held his shirts and rifled through a few of them. He suddenly realized that he was experiencing the unique pleasure of picking out the outfit that he would be buried in. He wondered jovially if he should wear a suit. He thought no. A flannel would suffice. He did put on one of his slightly nicer pairs of shoes. He grabbed a pair of sunglasses to shield his sensitive eyes from the insensitive sun and a jacket to shield him from the cold. He walked out of the room with purpose and a pack of cigarettes.

Chester and Arch were either still asleep or were awake in their rooms and had not found the strength or reason to step out into the world after the events of the night before. He was happy about this. His decision was final. He was not going to be swayed. But he did not want to explain it to anyone. Frankly, he did not want to speak to anyone at all. He sauntered up to the couch and gently slid the map out from behind it. The world seemed to shudder.

Damien held the map by its frame and moved promptly to the front door of the apartment. There was no use in wasting time. He opened the door, and as he did, he heard another door creak open behind him. He turned and saw Chester standing there in his boxers, wiping the sleep from his eyes.

"Damien," he said, pausing, "I am so ineffably sorry about last night." It was not really Chester who needed to apologize.

"It's not really you who needs to apologize," Damien said. "But thank you."

There was another moment of silence, and then Damien simply said, "I am going to the park."

Chester frowned a little, set his jaw, and curled his lips in. He cocked his head to the right like a curious, little Australian shepherd. He looked at the map in Damien's hands and raised his brow. He was hoping Damien would say more, but he did not.

"Okay," Chester said, deciding against saying more, obliviously damning humanity. Damien turned and walked out the door.

Damien needed to ensure that the entire map was covered in dirt all at once. A wheelbarrow could make this happen. He loaded the map into the back of his car, gently leaning it against the seats, and then got in himself. He put the car in drive, en route to the hardware store, keeping his eye on the map in the rearview mirror nearly the entire time.

As he walked the aisles, he once again wondered if the shoppers there knew what he was up to. He wondered if, in any way, he looked like he was purchasing tools to destroy all of humanity. He found a wheelbarrow and inspected it a bit. He lifted it, pulled it backward, and pushed it forward a few times. He set it back down and looked at the wheel, unsure exactly why he did that. He supposed he just wanted to make sure this went as well as the destruction of humanity could go. He did not want to fail the end of the world.

He picked up the wheelbarrow and pushed it to the shovels nearby. He found a sturdy one with a wood handle and threw it in the wheelbarrow. It made a loud clanging sound, and a woman nearby looked at him and smiled. She would not smile if she knew. He realized that no one knew. He realized that no one suspected him of anything because no one knew this was even possible. He was special. He stood apart. He was elevated. He was Damien, destroyer of worlds.

He purchased his wares and smiled at the cashier. She smiled back. He was starting to enjoy his dirty little secret.

An army of thick clouds had long since covered the sun to which he had awoken. The sky was greyed and looked like it was getting ready to fall. Perhaps it might snow.

Damien loaded the wheelbarrow and shovel into the front seat of his car. They barely fit. He had to twist them and push a bit and was afraid he would jostle the map too much and make another mark on the earth before the final one. He could not let this happen. Damien carefully loaded the car and got in himself. He adjusted the rearview to make sure that he could clearly view the map. It sneered at him from the backseat.

"You don't even know what's coming to you," he said out loud, wondering if the map could talk. He wondered if it could hear him. He wondered if it thought it was in control or if it thought that he was. He wondered if it was scared. Before he knew it, he looked up and saw that he was pulling into the parking lot of Broad Ripple Park.

He decided not to dally for fear that he may lose his nerve. He got out of the car and removed the shovel and wheelbarrow first. Then he placed the map carefully in the wheelbarrow. It did not fit perfectly so he had to set it carefully over the top. He did not like how much he was jostling the map. He reminded himself that it would all be over soon. With the shovel in his right hand alongside the right handle of the wheelbarrow, he began walking. He went as far from the parking lot as he could in the small park, past the far edge of a small running path that was there. Anyone brave enough to be running in the cold would only be able to see him at a distance. Not many people were out because of the weather, but he did not want to risk it. This would be the spot. He stopped walking and looked down at the ground. He pictured a gravestone there that read:

"Here lies humanity: God's most beautiful mistake."

Damien laid the map faceup carefully on the ground and began to dig, taking this time to consider the nature of mistakes. He thought about his actions in the godheart and the necessity of his folly. Without it, he would have never been allowed to dance like he did. He would have never been moved to tears in that holy place. His mistakes, his folly, were crucial to education and understanding, and folly requires action. Whether he was confident in his decisions or not, he needed to act. Then he would be led to discovery. Increasingly, as the hole deepened, he became resolute in the necessity of mistakes. He became sure that we just needed to act wildly and do everything to find out what not to do. He was sure he did not know. He was sure that he was unsure. He was sure he should do things in ignorant bliss.

With each breach of the shovel into the cold, hard earth, he felt more confidence in his decision. He stabbed the metal edge hard into the earth again and again. It felt good to be sure of something. He was sure that humanity was fallen. He was sure that it was a beautiful, pivotal mistake. But he could no longer live in a world where this map existed. No one could or should. Only trouble would come. Time and time again, trouble would come. To live in that reality would be long, slow, eternal torture. The map needed to be buried, never to be found again, alongside the ones that would inevitably use it so poorly. The mistake needed to be rectified, but it was good to know.

Almost in response to Damien's shoveling, it began to snow. This was not like the light flurries they had seen so far that strange winter. Large snowflakes swirled around him, creating a lovely winter scene. The earth was giving Damien one last show of beauty in hope of convincing him to alter his course, but he was sure. The snow whipped around him and began to accumulate a bit on the cold ground. A few snowflakes found their way to the surface of the upwards-facing map on the ground and entered it. All across the globe, giant snowflakes appeared in the sky. Some appeared in warmer climates and instantly turned to water for the heat, dropping a flood upon the earth below. Some remained frozen and buried the land in mountains of freshly falling snow. Bangalore, Vancouver, Addis Adaba, Berlin, Boulder, Seoul, Lima – place after place was covered in a varied form of precipitation.

Over the course of a few minutes, he filled the wheelbarrow far over its brim. It was time. A crown of sweat was forming around his head. This was for all of humanity. This was for Madeleine. This was for all his friends. This was for Chester, Arch, Erin, even that beloved scoundrel, Peter. He would save them all from themselves. He lit a cigarette. Like a man standing blindfolded in front of a firing squad, he would go down enjoying one last carnal pleasure. But this was also unlike that. This was a special circumstance. He was both the man and the firing squad.

Damien maneuvered the wheelbarrow so that the front of it was facing the map lying upwards on the ground. Next, he tensed the muscles in his back and arms and began to pull the handles upward. Goodbye, cruel world. His resolve was sound. His intention to send the payload toward the map was secure.

But before Damien's dirty airstrike left the wheelbarrow, time slowed until it reached a standstill. Damien froze. The impending doom of humanity sat in the wheelbarrow, looming above the map for one suspended moment. This could not be. A voice that was supposed to be wiped from existence rang out across the stillness:

"Damien!"

CHAPTER 28:

THE TRUTH RUNS THROUGH

MADELEINE SAT IN A place of transition, a place where people never stayed. They only came and went, hurriedly passing through on their way to bigger and brighter places. She inhaled. It smelled too clean. There was no semblance of permanence in the scent that greeted her nostrils. There was no lived-in feeling. There was only movement and transience. It made her feel uncertain and uncomfortable. She missed Damien. He always seemed so steady, so sure. She missed feeling safe and secure with him at home. She missed her pilot light.

As Madeleine sat at the gate awaiting the boarding call for her redeye flight to Portland, she thought about things that Damien used to say. She thought about his insistence on believing in and embracing both sides of life: the good and the bad. This whole situation was undoubtedly bad. In fact, it was the worst thing that had ever happened to them. This map was assumedly the worst thing that had ever happened to anyone. But he could not embrace it. He could not embrace her infidelity. How could he embrace it? Why would he embrace it? She had betrayed him. The map had betrayed all of them. She felt her humanity weigh heavy on her shoulders, and she stared at her shoes. The left one was untied.

What she had done was so hateful. She was afraid. She was sure that she had ruined the love that they had. She was so horribly human. Damien was also human. And with that thought, she realized that Damien may have been wrong. He was close, but he was wrong.

When the cup is half- or more than half-empty, there had to be a good way to handle it. Maybe the key was not to embrace the bad but to endure the bad. The key was to have the foresight to know that bad was bound to happen, acknowledge that it had happened when it did, and then keep going. Maybe that was what he was trying to say the whole time, but he was limited and could not say it the way she needed to hear it. He could not say things perfectly all the time. He could not understand everything. He was bound to break when things went bad, and when he did, it was her job to pick up the pieces. He had failed her in telling her everything was fine. She had failed him in kissing Peter. He had failed her by not forgiving, for not choosing to endure the bad with her. Then she failed him again by leaving. It was failure across the board because they were human, but they needed to keep going.

She was going to make him practice what he had tried to preach all those years. She was going to make him "embrace the bad" and then endure it. But she was going to make him embrace and endure that bad with her there. She refused to accept their separation. She could be his strength when he needed it. He had certainly been hers more times than she could count. There was bad, and there was good. There was hate, and there was love. They weren't going to give up simply because they experienced one of them that they did not usually see together. That was poppycock.

Some things are impossible to know. It is impossible to know if good and bad are things that come from humans or from somewhere else, but the fact stands that they exist. Good and bad both exist. They may not both need to be celebrated, and they may not both need to be loathed, but they both needed to be experienced and endured. Her mind took her back to one particular evening when she and Damien were lying intertwined in bed. He had looked up from his journal at her with his sad, pensive eyes and talked to her about truth.

"The truth runs through us, Madeleine, not from us."

"Why do you say that?"

"There's just no way it could be from us. It certainly isn't coming from me at my particular point in time here after millions of years of life and men much smarter than me. There's no way I'm coming up with anything original. I'm just lucky enough to tap into it from time to blessed time." He rambled on about this for a while. "We're mere witnesses as it passes by, like happy families at a parade. It has to come from somewhere else. People are too tainted and… stupid," he chuckled, "to be responsible for truth."

He spoke about truth as if it was something witnessed but in which he played no part. And he seemed fine with this fact. He sounded like he hoped not to grasp it, not to hold it, only to stand its courts, knowing that if he did grasp it, tainted by his hands, it would cease to be. But standing in the courts of something as beautiful as truth compels a man to act. The heart of God cannot be traveled without reaction.

But it must be traveled without reaction, Madeleine thought. As the parade passes by, a person has to fight their impulse to run into the middle of the merry progression. They simply have to cheer as it passes by. They cannot stop the parade. Madeleine was adding thoughts to Damien's original one, coming to a new, more complex understanding that could not be accomplished in the mind of one man. Even miles away, they worked well together.

Maybe love and hate, good and bad were not sourced in humanity either. She had already established that love and hate were both realities that must be dealt with. They were both truth, and if that was accurate, by way of Damien's theory, love and hate might come from somewhere else entirely. They flowed through humanity, not from. They were simply things in which people get to take part, not things that they create.

And if love flows through, not from, Madeleine realized she may be able to grab hold of it again. There was no doubt that she had momentarily lost her grasp of it, and that fact saddened her. But that sadness was beginning to wash away. Now she began to believe there was a chance that she could find a new way to grab hold again. It was never hers in the first place. She borrowed it once, and she may be allowed to borrow it again.

And if love was not something she spawned, she could not ruin it. It would continue to flow to and from other places despite her best efforts to ruin. Unless she found its source and poisoned that, she could not ruin love, and she could not ruin truth. Pure truth would still flow from the source and offer her the opportunity to bathe in it again. She simply needed to find a new channel. The channel she had been using was done. Anything that flowed from that anymore would be poisoned, but there was so much opportunity in thinking about truth this way. There were other channels. There was an untainted source. She felt excitement climb her spine and ignite her skin. Her hope was now in something besides herself. The truth runs through.

"Let it run through me," she prayed.

And just like that, with a simple change in perspective, a rope ladder called hope was dropped into the pit that she had dug for herself and into which she had descended. She firmly grasped it and began to climb.

Madeleine reached down and tied her shoe.

CHAPTER 29:

THE SECOND-TO-LAST CHAPTER

MADELEINE SNATCHED HER BAGS from the floor of the terminal and raced toward the airport exit as fast as her legs could carry her. She was going to endure, with Damien, anything that came their way. Where all was once lost, there was now hope. She called for an Uber from the terminal. When the app asked for her destination, she paused. She wanted to go straight to him, but it was far too late. She decided to go home and find him early in the morning.

Behind her, a television screen displayed the national news, and a small crowd was gathering beneath it. The sound was off, but the anchor seemed to be speaking earnestly. The ticker at the bottom of the screen reported hundreds of thousands dead in Portland. The city had been wiped entirely from the face of the earth in a burst of flame just moments before. The heads of the gathering crowd turned back and forth following the ticker. They sobbed. They gasped. They prayed for the world not to end. She did not see any of it.

Madeleine made it home safe and sound after a long Uber. All she could think about was Damien during the trip. She was sure that they were going to be okay. They were going to make it. She laid her head against her pillow and fell asleep quickly, faster than she had in days. She felt peace.

That night Madeleine had a dream. It was a dream with no events, no passing of time, almost no content at all. But she remembered feeling warm as the night passed by.

The next morning she got up and raced to the boys' apartment. She bounded up the steps to their front door and began pounding. The door swung open, and she was greeted by Chester in his boxers, eating a bowl of cereal. He smiled from ear to ear, dropped his bowl of cereal to the ground, and reached forward to hug her. Madeleine was alive. Their feet were splashed by milk and Fruity Pebbles. He pulled back, still grinning like an idiot, and shouted for Arch, who still had not emerged from his room. She looked him up and down and smiled a little because he was eating cereal in his underwear.

"You have no idea how good it is to see you. I guess you didn't make it to Portland." He shouted for Arch again. There was no stir from Arch's bedroom. "Did you—"

"That's a good look," she said, cutting him off. He smiled a little and nodded. "I'm looking for Damien."

"I would imagine you are," he replied. "He's going to lose his mind when he sees you. He just left a little bit ago."

"Well, tool, where did he go?"

"He said he was going to the park."

"Broad Ripple Park?"

"I would imagine."

"Thanks!" she shouted as she turned and jumped down the steps to leave.

"Hey! Madeleine!"

"Yes, Chester?"

"Damien took the map with him."

Her heart somersaulted within her chest. She turned again to run toward her car, this time with a bit more haste.

"Hey! Madeleine!"

"What, Chester!?" She turned again to face him, standing there in his underwear, socks soaked by cereal milk.

"It's really good to see you."

She paused. "It's good to see you too."

She turned a final time, sprinting again toward her car. The shoe-strings of her heart were quickly retied by her reclaimed optimism. A smile returned to her face. It was a radiant smile. It was the smile that had so many times brightened the lives of their little group. It was a smile that she would share with Damien to show him that the truth runs through and that they may find love again. Her tanned skin made her smile shine even brighter in her mouth. It was truly a beacon of hope.

Madeleine had never felt so much joy in hope in her life, and that was saying something. She was going to find Damien, and everything was going to be fine. They were going to find a new channel of love and let it take them. Chester's words played on a loop in her head: *He's going to lose his mind when he sees you.* She hoped that he did. Their minds had gotten them into so much trouble thus far. It began snowing as she got closer to the park.

Madeleine pulled into the parking lot and drove the car sideways across two separate parking spots. She was too excited to try to park accurately. She ran from the car and into the park. Luckily, it was small. After running back and forth for a minute past the few sad souls brave enough to be out at the park in such cold – a few couples walking and one bundled man working out – she saw him. He was lighting a cigarette, standing next to a wheelbarrow full of dirt. Snow whipped around him and landed in his long, greasy hair.

"Damien!" she shouted as she began running toward him. He did not turn. He must not have heard. He picked the wheelbarrow up and turned it toward something lying on the ground. She got closer. Her heart dropped into the pit of her stomach. It was the map.

In a swift, decisive motion, Damien pulled the handles of the wheel-barrow upward. Madeleine witnessed this in horror.

"Damien!" she screamed again.

This time he turned. The vision of Madeleine sucker punched him, and he drew as much cold air into his lungs as they could hold. Time stopped for a moment as they looked at each other. She was alive, and she was there. Damien had heard that he would see the faces of the ones he loved in the moments before death, but he was sure that he would only ever see this face again in his mind. For a moment, he tussled with believing that she was actually there. He prayed it was more than a hallucination. He needed to believe that she was there. In the last moments of his life, he wanted to hope.

Damien melted. Her visage, once again, like it had done so many times before, took his resolve and dissolved it. Madeleine felt him melt and knew there could be love again. They wanted to live. They wanted to love, together. A nearly tangible wash of regret, apology, and forgiveness word-lessly flowed from each of them to the other, and they felt purified, whiter than the snow that fell around them. They wanted nothing of themselves individually. They, again, wanted for themselves collaboratively. At the final intersection, in their own respective vehicles, they both accelerated and collided in the middle, destroying their own desires, trajectories, themselves as separate entities, with no intention or idea of how or where they would go next. In the middle, they combined and lost themselves, their hearts aligning once again and for the last time into one and in the name of something beyond themselves: love.

Damien wanted to take it back. He wanted to undo what he had done. He wanted to hold Madeleine and hurt with her. He wanted them all to hurt. But as Arch would say, "You can't unring a bell."

In its usual behavior, time continued. Its momentary delay proved to be nothing more than an illusion caused by regret, desire, dramatic effect. Madeleine's hand stretched forward, Damien's arms flew upward, and the dirt resumed its journey toward the map. One solitary, long-overdue tear formed in the corner of Damien's eye.

And above every city, state, and province; every county, country, and continent; above the First Church of the Finger of God; and across the entirety of the earth, the sky turned pitch-black, and without warning and wrought by the hand of a sad, contemplative musician in Indianapolis, each living thing and square foot of terrestrial surface was crushed under billions of tons of fertile soil.

CHAPTER 30:

...

WHO KNOWS WHAT GROWS?